THE WICKED WITCH

THE OBSIDIAN SPINDLE SAGA

BOOK TWO

RUSSELL NOHELTY

SPECIAL THANKS

Adriane Ruzak, Amanda Jackson, Angela, Anthony Bachman, Caledonia, Caspar Williams, Celeste and Bryan Cornish, Chad Bowden, Chris Call, Chris Meeson, Christopher C Epping, Christopher Prew, CJ Ives Lopez, Daniel Biittner, Daniel Groves, Dave Baxter, Dave Goldberg, David Chamberlain, David Drummond, David Straube, Desiree Duffy, DJ Inzeo, Ed S, Edward Nycz Jr., Emerson Kasak, Erin Congdon, Gabriella Farmer, Gary Phillips, Hannah Long, Hollie Buchanan II, Jeff Lewis, Jennifer & Charlie Geer, John C. Heller, Johnny Britt, Jon Tugan, Joshua Bowers, Joshua Pantalleresco, Juli, Kimberly Herout, Larry Gilman, Lincoln City Archery, Lisa Homolka, Lisa Lyons, Matthew Johnson, Maxi Organ, Melissa Showers, Michael Kingston, Michael Perler, Mike Jones, Monkey King Comics, Nic Nelson, Nick Smith, Paul Rose Jr., Per Stalby, Rachel Adams, Rhel ná DecVandé, Richard A Williams, Rob MacAndrew, Rowan, S.A. McClure, Salvatore Puma, Scott Kilburn, Stephen Ballentine, Steven "Waffles" Lane, Taiga Char, Talinda Willard (everfai), Victoria Nohelty, and Walter Weiss

The Wicked Witch
Book 2 of the Obsidian Spindle Saga

By:
Russell Nohelty
Edited by:
Leah Lederman

Proofread by:
Katrina Roets

Cover by:
JV Arts

Formatting by:
Turbo Kitten Industries

CHAPTER 1

NIMUE

I'm cold.

I flew for the better part of the day and late into the following evening after being chased out of Oz by the whelp queen Rose. The wind stung against my face until I shook all over from the chill, but I dared not stop for even a moment until I reached Hera's keep far above the forests of the Dark Domain.

I could not risk traveling by foot for fear of being arrested. Even if my troops pledged fealty to me, I feared that their loyalties would now switch to the new queen. Teleporting would have brought me to Hera's castle more quickly; too quickly, actually. I had failed to keep her prize and feared her rash temper. I needed to give her a chance to cool down so she wouldn't pull me limb from limb the instant I showed up.

Ungrateful usurpers had no respect for what I'd built over the last century as the queen of Oz. I spent every waking hour in service to those ignorant hayseeds, and they had no appreciation for what I had done for them.

Having my own subjects scream for my head was truly the end all of a rotten day.

The citizens of the Emerald City cheered my defeat as if I was a monster, and not their liberator. I would have brought them all with me back to Earth. We would have left the Dream Realm behind had I found a way through the Obsidian Spindle, but that wasn't enough for Ozma or her sycophants. Ozma had no vision, except to sow deceit. She turned the whole city against me. Her ilk turned Rose—the Dreamer—and the Gorgon against me, and now, I was a queen without a land to rule.

Hera gave me her blessing, but not control over her Dark Domain. Most gods of Urgu had no interest in ruling their kingdom, but Hera was a micromanager. She needed to bend every blade of grass to her will...and did not abide failure. In the hundreds of years I worked in her service, she killed many for less.

I don't even know how I failed. It all happened in a blur. One instant, my men were opening a portal back to Earth using the Dreamer's soul to power our machine. The power of the Dreamer was working. I could feel the veil between our worlds breaking apart, and then in the next instant, Hypnos gave his blessing to that silly little girl, and she cast me out of the castle.

I looked back at the Gates of Droangor, which separated Hypnos's land from Hera's and the other gods: the Sandlands, where Sekhmet's people roamed; the Mountains, where Agrona ruled; the Bogs of Insanity, where Loki kept council, and the Thatch, where Anansi kept his home.

In the distance, The Emerald City shone brightly over the Land of Oz, and behind it, the Obsidian Spindle stood tall, its gnarled black spire pointing high into the sky. It was there that the fates spun the destiny of men and protected the only door out of the Dream Realm back to Earth. One day that most precious resource would be in my control. I would unlock its secrets and find my way back to Earth. It was the only shred of hope I had left.

I looked across Hera's Dark Domain and saw her keep, high atop the tallest hill. It was there I had received Hera's blessing, and plotted to overthrow Ozma and rule the Land of Oz. Hera's palace was where I kept my library, filled with the forgotten knowledge of Urgu. It was where I learned how to overthrow a queen and so I was returning so that I could plot my comeback.

The Land of Oz had hope now, in the Dreamer and her harem of misguided idealists. If I wasn't careful, that hope could spread throughout Urgu. Hypnos made sure of that when he adorned her with his blessing and brought his magic back to the world. For decades, his magic had faded from the Dream Realm, making my plans easier to enact. Now, I would require Hera's full force and support if I were to be successful. Somehow I would destroy Rose and her ilk once and for all.

To reach Hera's castle, it was necessary to climb a sheer rock face. She did not want visitors. Her subjects lived in constant fear of her, which made ruling her kingdom all the easier. She did not care if they lived or died. She only cared about one thing: escaping her prison and finally returning to the universe once again. Any other purpose was inconsequential, which is why we worked so well together.

Her castle was made from the same obsidian that forged the Spindle. Hera insisted on it, even though it meant the death of five thousand dwarves when they mined the ore from the deepest caves in Urgu and carried it up the mountain by hand. Obsidian was one of the few objects in the universe which could not be affected by magic. That was precisely what made the Obsidian Spindle impervious to my efforts to open it, and to Hera's repeated attempts to destroy it. When Hera made her own castle, she demanded the same level of invulnerability.

Even the Queen's castle in The Emerald City was not so impermeable as Hera's lair. Hypnos had created magical wards to bar Hera from coming and going as she pleased. During my reign I had disabled or reduced many of them to allow Hera and her shadow demons through my halls. Every piece of information about the wards was locked up in my library vault, and I killed anyone who knew anything about them, but I knew the Dreamer brat and her merry band would surely find a way to reinstate the protections against me and Hera.

I had to find a way back to the castle, and through the Obsidian Spindle, before the magical wards were raised again. Our retaliation must be swift and brutal.

The black shutters above Hera's throne room were open when I reached the castle. She knew I was coming.

Of course she knew that I was coming.

She was a god. There was not much in Urgu that she couldn't predict. Perhaps the last thing that truly surprised her was the return of Hypnos's power to the land, and how quickly the Dreamer used it to cast her out of the Emerald City.

The moment I flew through the windows they slammed closed behind me, and I fell to the ground, tumbling on the plush carpet in front of Hera's throne. Blue lights flickered along every wall, but otherwise the room was dark, which was how Hera wanted it. She could move freely through the shadows. In all my decades in her service, I had only seen her true form twice.

"You have failed me," Hera's stern voice boomed. Her

violet eyes blinked in front of me, and that was all of her that I saw in the dark.

"I'm sorry, my queen. You must know that I tried my best. You couldn't expect me to know—"

"Silence!" Hera shouted. "I do not wish to hear your excuses."

"I'm sorry, your majesty."

"Yes," Hera replied with venom in her voice. "You are, aren't you? You are sorry for your existence."

I looked up, trying in vain to meet Hera's eyes. "You must know that I couldn't predict Hypnos coming back. Even you, in all your greatness, couldn't foresee that."

"Hrm."

I balled my fists up under me. "We were so close to victory, my queen. I believe that if we can simply retake the Emerald Ci—"

"There is no *simply* now, Nimue!" Hera roared. "Nothing is simple with the return of Hypnos. I told you to act quicker, but you chose to delay."

I bit the side of my lip, trying to control my anger at her accusation. She would not tolerate insolence, and my voice could not betray me. "It was not my choice. The pieces had to fall into place, and they had, your majesty. We were mere moments from glorious victory."

Hera sighed. "And yet, you ended up failing me in the most awful way possible. Not only did you fail to open a portal to Earth, but you also brought the magic of Hypnos back to this land. Unacceptable."

"Please," I begged. "Give me another chance."

"Why?"

I took a deep breath. *Project confidence.* "Because I am your best chance of getting back to Earth and you know it."

Her purple eyes blinked open and shot toward me. "If

that is true, then there truly is no hope. Goodbye, Nimue. May your failures haunt you all your remaining days."

Before I could speak, Hera snapped her fingers and the blackness collapsed around me. I drifted away. The last thing I saw was a sly smile cracking through the darkness under Hera's eyes. She was savoring the moment of my banishment.

CHAPTER 2
ROSE

"Ow!" I shouted as Chelle's blast singed my hand for the second time in the last hour. The throne room had become our makeshift training academy where we practiced magic between the stream of well-wishers waiting to kiss the ring of the new queen—me.

I hated the throne room. Every moment I spent there was an unwelcome one. Nimue, the despot queen who ruled before me, wanted to project an element of fear in any who entered and so she kept the place dark and menacing. Thick black tapestries blocked the light from the stained-glass windows behind the throne.

Since I took over the throne, at least, I had insisted the floor-to-ceiling windows leading to the balcony remain open at all times. I used them to look out upon the Emerald City, and the Land of Oz. Even in the rain, the breeze brought the warmth of nature into a castle that for too long had been cold and hollow.

I turned my face from the wind and gave Chelle an eyebrow. "Go easy on me, all right?"

She laughed. I loved her laugh, even when it was mocking me. "I'm sorry. It's just—you're so bad at this."

She was having a ball teaching me magic. For most of our relationship, she was the gorgon with incredible magical powers and I was just the normal by her side, but now we both had magic; I had recently been blessed by the god Hypnos himself and charged with carrying out his will on Urgu.

Unfortunately, Hypnos vanished into the ether before he could teach me how to use my powers. I could not find, or feel him, anywhere in Urgu. I had to rely on Chelle to teach me. It was not going well.

"I'm not bad. I just don't understand. You're telling me to speak a bunch of gibberish and then my powers will work, but they just keep...not working."

"You'll get it," Chelle replied, walking toward me.

I shook my head. "I doubt it. You're a terrible teacher."

Chelle picked up my singed hand and kissed it, the snakes on her head cooing sympathetically. "Better?" she asked.

"No," I chuckled. "Too bad you didn't learn any healing magic."

The snakes on her gorgon head flicked my arm with their forked tongues. Even little Albie, our old favorite snake who had lost a tooth, seemed happy, despite the fact that Chelle was miserable in Urgu and had been ever since we arrived a month ago.

We locked eyes for a moment, then Chelle said, "I just like smashing things too much to bother with healing."

I wrapped my arms around her and kissed her deeply. I could feel the sadness coursing through her. She hated Urgu. She wanted nothing more than to go back to Earth, but in the weeks since we'd banished the Wicked Witch, we hadn't gotten any closer to finding a way to open the Obsidian Spindle and speak with the fates. They were the only ones who could send us home.

Of course, I wasn't trying that hard to open the tower. I was perfectly happy as the Queen of Oz. Back on Earth, I was just a girl in a coma, a nothing burger from nowheresville; here in Urgu, I was one of the god-touched, and arguably the most powerful one, since my power came from the god of dreams, Hypnos, rightful ruler of the Dream Realm. Here, I had magic. Here, people looked up to me.

"Are you hungry?" I asked Chelle as she walked me back toward the gnarled black throne that Nimue vacated after we defeated her. In time, I hoped to learn how to bend the metal to my will, as she and Ozma had before me, but I hadn't been able to figure out the right spell yet. Chelle couldn't help because she was only skilled in offensive magic, not transfiguration.

If I didn't learn how to unlock my more powerful magic soon, then we risked another invasion, and my inevitable death at the hands of Nimue's formidable abilities. She'd had hundreds of years to develop her powers. I'd had a few weeks. I hated even more my lack of progress since that initial conflict. Part of me wished that Nimue would return, so I could feel the anger swell through me again like it did during my first encounter with her. I wondered if that would unlock something within me and give me control of the awesome power Hypnos had entrusted with me.

"Have you had any luck contacting him?" Chelle asked.

"No," I said, letting go of her hand and climbing the stairs to my throne. "Wherever he came from, he seemed to return there once he blessed me." I sat down. The metal laid uncomfortably beneath me, and the seat numbed my legs after only a couple of minutes. I hated the throne more than Chelle hated Urgu.

Unfortunately, I was stuck there sometimes eight hours a day, as people from all over the kingdom came to bend the knee and swear fealty to me. Their hollow platitudes were welcome, but they came from fear—fear of my power, which meant that I had to reflect power lest they realized I was unable to force their allegiance.

I had no interest in doing so. Fear might have worked for Nimue, but I had no desire to rule by it. Before Ozma disintegrated in a pile of dust, she told me that her goal for the kingdom was to bring equality to all her people, noble and peasant alike, and introduce technology into the world so they could move past their medieval era and into the industrial revolution and beyond.

I came from a world full of technology, and I could help people move into the future. But I knew I wouldn't be able to do so if the denizens of Urgu feared me. I needed them to embrace the new world I planned to build. If they didn't, I would be deposed, like the nobles had deposed Ozma before me. I had to show them the way into the future was best for all of us.

The horns blew outside the throne room and I placed my head in my hands. "Christ. Can I get not one moment's peace?"

"What?" Chelle said with a smile. "You're popular. You're the Kristen Chenowith here, just like you wanted."

"I don't get it."

"When we get back to Earth, I'll take you to see *Wicked*. You'll love it. After this whole thing, it will probably even have a deeper meaning."

She insisted I was going back to Earth with her, despite my constant objections to the contrary.

A young squire rushed into the throne room. His puffy black and green shirt was embossed with a peacock, the sign of Hera and sigil of the Wicked Witch. I hadn't had time to choose a new uniform, so they all wore the garb of Hera and Nimue. It made me uneasy every time I saw it.

"Your majesty, your majesty," the squire said in a thick cockney accent. "A guest comes to have an audience with you."

"Who is it?" I asked, sitting as straight and regally as possible.

"Your grace, she says she's Queen Aine, the fairy queen from the Enchanted Woods."

"The queen of the Unseelie? Here!" Chelle said, her hands glowing with flames. "Send her away before I blow her to bits."

"No!" I shouted. "That would cause an incident. She is one of my subjects, and I am obligated to speak with her. I might need her help in the days to come."

Chelle whipped around to face me. "You can't be serious."

I nodded. "As a heart attack. Show her in."

CHAPTER 3
CHELLE

How many times can you tell your girlfriend she was making a dumb mistake before you just stood back, smiled, and let her make it?

Ten?

Twenty?

A hundred?

Rose was the queen after all, and even though the whole castle was still draped in the tapestry and colors of the wicked witch, Rose tried her best to act like she was in charge. It wasn't working. The level of indignation permeating through every meeting Rose took could be cut with a rusty butter knife.

Of course, it wasn't easy for her. Rose wasn't decisive, or much of a leader. She had many wonderful qualities, but steadfast determination wasn't one of them, nor was faking bravery in the face of the unknown. Nobody expected Rose to slip seamlessly into the job after a single month, but they did expect a certain level of confidence.

Before she met me, Rose had drifted through most of

her life just trying to keep her head above water. I wasn't a bastion of rock-solid strength, but I gave her something to latch onto in the ferocious storm that was her life, even if I was sinking, too. Rose, for her part, prevented me from drowning in the torrent of pressure that smashed against me every moment of every day. Somehow, together, we buoyed each other up. Both of us were flawed, broken, and incomplete, but somehow, together we formed a singular, functional human. She became the warm, loving caretaker I never had in my youth, and I became the protector she needed against enemies big and small.

It wasn't a perfect system, but it was one that worked for us. Or it did, before Urgu. Now, it splintered and fractured under our new roles. I could only protect her so much. She still had to be out in front, leading, and every time she let go of my hand and took the throne, my heart jumped into my throat.

Her being queen forced us into a different dynamic, and that was a bitter pill. She was the queen, and though we used to make decisions together, deferring to whoever had the stronger opinion, now every decision boiled down to her decision, even if it was misguided or foolish.

Who was I to argue? I was just a gorgon monster. Even the fact I was allowed in the castle had caused a mini scandal among the royal court.

Rose was queen of the Emerald City, the capital of the Land of Oz, the most important land in all of Urgu because it housed the Obsidian Spindle. The fates were the most powerful beings in the Dream Realm aside from Hypnos—the only ones with the power to send someone back to Earth—and they lived there.

I couldn't call her out in front of the whole kingdom

without fracturing her tenuous grasp on power and threatening my precarious acceptance among the courtesans. Even though I kept my distaste for her policies to the confines of our bedroom, it rocked our foundation. She wanted so badly to matter, and now she mattered so much that all eyes were on her, and I feared she would break under the pressure.

If only I could find a way to open the Obsidian Spindle and speak to the fates this could all be fixed. Rose and I could go home and in time her memories of this place would fade. We could carve out a life for ourselves, together, away from the madness of Urgu.

Every hour I was away from Rose's side I spent rummaging through the library, though my attempts at searching for answers were in vain. I was no closer to finding a way to open the door, and without access to the Spindle, I could not petition the fates to get us back to Earth. Without a break soon, I feared that Rose and I would splinter and crack until we drifted apart forever.

In the meantime, Rose was in danger. She needed a lot of training before she could wield her newfound powers, but I wasn't much of a trainer. She had regressed since the night she banished the Wicked Witch Nimue, and if she didn't soon learn how to control the awesome powers bestowed to her by Hypnos, then Nimue would surely return, more powerful than ever, and destroy her like she had destroyed Ozma.

Pastiche, the tubby herald, ran his stubby legs into the throne room. Two bugle players stepped inside the grand entrance and lined the edges of the grand doorway that reached nearly to the top of the painted ceiling, decorated with twisted visions of monsters and fairies torn limb from limb on a bloody battlefield.

Once the bugle players were locked into position, two more stepped inside, and then two others, until a dozen bugle players lined each side of the room.

"Your royal highness," Pastiche shouted. "May I present Queen Aine of the Enchanted Woods, regent of the Forbidden Forest, Protectors of Fairy Kind, and Royal Duchess of the Unseelie."

My jaw clenched. I did not like Queen Aine. The last time we met, she imprisoned both me and my companion Red and used Rose in an experiment to destroy the veil between the Dream Realm and Earth. Only a daring escape from our cell saved us and Rose from certain death at the hands of the fairy queen.

There were two kinds of fairies: the kind-hearted Seelie, and the dreadfully wicked Unseelie. Queen Aine was the bad kind—the only kind left after she murdered the Seelie and took control of the Woods. There was no good in her heart, though I wondered if any queen could be truly good while they sat upon the throne.

I looked up at Rose, her back straight, feigning the strength she desperately wished she could project. Her right pinky tapped the edge of the black throne faster and faster as her panic grew, yet her face remained stoic.

I didn't want her to be strong. Her power was in her vulnerability. She was open and fragile and even after a few weeks on the throne I could see her new position chiseling that from her and replacing it with the hardness that a queen must possess.

Four silver, glittering fairies flew into the room carrying

a golden palanquin between them. They were three apples high or slightly shorter. However, they held themselves with such power and confidence that it seemed like nothing could hurt them.

Without a word, the silver fairies placed the palanquin down and pulled open the pink curtain along its side. A faint purple glow emanated from inside of the chariot and lit the black carpet with the queen's glow. From behind the curtain, a purple fairy burst forth, shimmering brighter than her palanquin bearers, wearing a golden headdress adorned with jewels, and trailing a pink cape behind her.

"My queen," the fairy said, flying toward the throne. "What a great honor it is to see you."

"Stop right there, Queen Aine!" I shouted, stepping into her path. My eyes burned with fire. "You are no friend to the realm or its protector."

Queen Aine snarled. "How dare you speak to me this way?" She looked at Rose, who was seated on her throne, shifting uncomfortably. "I come in friendship and this is how you treat me?"

"You are no friend to us," I reiterated, sternly. "The last time—"

Queen Aine put up her hand and spoke over me. "I do not speak to commoners." She turned her head again to Rose. "This is not very queenly, your highness. I know you are new to the throne, which is the only reason why I let this slight stand without declaring war on the Emerald City. However, tell your witch not to address me again, or I shall take it as a great affront."

"You little b—" I snarled.

"Chelle!" Rose shouted. "That is enough."

I spun on her. "Are you kidding me?"

Rose's eyes went wide. I could sense her frantic, silent

begging. She pleaded wordlessly for me not to cause a scene. "That will be all. Step aside."

My face contorted in every direction, trying to hide my disgust and anger at Rose's decision. I had to be supportive. It was only for a little while. Soon I would find a way home for the both of us, and this nightmare would be over.

"That's better," Aine said with a slight smile.

"I'm very sorry for our rudeness," Rose said with a nod, annunciating each syllable. "It's been quite hectic here in the last days since—well, since the transition from Nimue."

The fairy queen floated forward. "I understand. After all, you haven't even had time to redecorate. Of course, that assumes you do not like these ghastly decorations. We fairies convey power with our actions, not the adornments of our castle."

Rose looked around at the hall. "Yes, it would be nice to get rid of this decor. Everywhere I look, I only see Nimue, and I am reminded of her trying to kill me...*twice* if I recall."

Rose emphasized the word "twice," making her implication clear to everybody in the room. She had not forgotten that Queen Aine had tried to kill her.

"I'm sorry for my part in all of that," Queen Aine replied, dropping her voice. "You must understand that the temptation to side with Nimue was great. However, since she has left the throne, it's like a great fog has lifted and my judgement has been restored."

Rose gave a slight, but careful smile. "That is nice to hear because we will not have any more of that unpleasantness moving forward. There will be no more breaking of the Veil, or siding with Hera's minions, yes?"

Aine nodded. "I can agree to that."

The Veil was the barrier between the Dream Realm, and the rest of the universe. The thin shield was how Urgu became a prison for gods who irritated the pantheons, and breaking through it became the great mission of Nimue, Hera, and her sycophants from the moment they realized they could not open the Obsidian Spindle and entreat with the fates themselves. Destroying the Veil would obliterate Urgu, and dreams, forever, leaving humanity with nothing left but nightmares for the rest of eternity.

Rose lifted her eyebrows in question. "So I can count on your allegiance?"

"You can." The fairy queen bowed her head.

I couldn't take it anymore. The vitriol boiled up through my stomach and out of my mouth. "And how can we trust you?"

"Whelp!" Aine barked.

"My apologies for Chelle's outburst," Rose said, directing the queen's attention back to her. "But she asks a good question. How can we assure your allegiance?"

"My loyalty has never been questioned before."

"What a load of crap," I whispered under my breath.

"Chelle," Rose said sternly. "Do not make me ask you to leave."

"You can't—" I started, but Rose held up her hand.

"However," Rose continued, staring daggers at the fairy queen. "I'm afraid I'll need some assurances from you."

Queen Aine held her hands out. "What can I give?"

Rose straightened her back in a regal show. "A show of support."

"What would you ask?"

"We know your people helped Nimue escape Oz. We want to know where she was headed."

Queen Aine thought for a moment, and then nodded. "Very well. But I would like to have your assurance that the

Enchanted Wood will remain under fairy control as long as you sit on the throne."

Rose stood up, and nearly looked foreboding. "I have no interest in your woods, except to ensure that travelers can pass through unmolested."

Queen Aine breathed deeply. "That will be hard to accomplish. My people—"

Rose held up her hand and finished Queen Aine's sentence. "Are under the protection of the crown, and the crown demands their devotion."

It was the most confident Rose had sounded since she sat on the throne, and it was hard for me not to grin with each passing word, especially as the scorn on Queen Aine's face grew more pronounced.

"I will tell my people that travelers are off limits, but if any seek us out, then I cannot guarantee their safety."

"Fair enough," Rose said, seating herself once more and gripping the edges of her throne. "Then you will have my protection until we can find Hypnos and bring him back. Then, it will be up to him to decide what to do with you."

"And is that your intention? To bring him back?"

"Of course. He is the rightful ruler of Urgu, and the only one powerful enough to keep the other gods in line."

The shadow left Queen Aine's face. "Very well. Your assurance is acceptable to me. Nimue wished to leave the Land of Oz and enter the sanctuary of Hera's kingdom in the Dark Domain. However, she knew she could never make it through the Gates of Droangor without capture, since the whole kingdom was on high alert. So, she asked me to bring her through the doors. Most magic cannot penetrate the Wall of Itherium that surrounds our kingdom, but fairy magic does, so we brought her through the gates, as a favor to an old friend. After that, we washed our hands of her, and turned our attention to helping the new queen."

"And we're just supposed to believe you?" I nearly spat.

Queen Aine turned to me. "I don't care what you believe, but to allay your fears I present a gift." She pressed her hands together and whispered an incantation under her breath. Then, she slapped her hands together and her hands glowed a bright yellow. A black key materialized between them.

"Do you know of Hera's library?" Queen Aine asked me.

I shook my head. "No."

"She has the greatest library in all of Urgu. It used to be rivaled by Hypnos's, but once he was gone and Nimue took control of Oz, she raided his library and took its greatest books to Hera's castle. In the back of that library, behind a locked door, rests the most powerful book in Urgu, bound in gold and forged from dreams. A book that can only be read by the one blessed by Hypnos, it contains the greatest secrets of the Dream Realm, including how to open the Obsidian Spindle. This key opens that door, and if you bring that book back to the Emerald City, your paramour can read it. In fact, she is the only one who can."

I stepped forward, watching Rose, whose brows were furrowed with dread. I knew she sensed, just as I did, that this was a trick from the Unseelie queen, but it was also an answer to the puzzle that plagued my every hour in Urgu, and now I was given a way to end it all. To what end was unclear, but to an end, and that was more hope than I had since the night the Wicked Witch was defeated.

"And you will give it to us?" I asked.

"As a coronation gift," Queen Aine said.

"Coronation?" Rose asked.

"Of course." The fairy paused. "Have you not planned your coronation yet?"

"I mean," Rose said, shifting in her seat. "I...am the queen. I'm sitting on the throne. So, I figured..."

Queen Aine placed the key in my hand and flew toward Rose. "No, no, no. You must make a show of power to demonstrate, without a doubt, that you are the true queen. Nobody in Oz will accept you as their queen until the coronation has been given by the High Majesty Pious of the Church of the Six. Has nobody told you that? What of your advisors?"

"My...advisors...don't know much about the royal court, unfortunately. They barely look at me, except to sing my praises and then vanish back to their homes."

"No, no, no. This will not do." Queen Aine paused for a moment. "I will grant you a second gift, which is my council in this trying time."

"You want to advise the queen?" I said.

"Well, somebody has to. She can't keep taking advice from uncultured swine like you. She won't last another month."

"And she'll last longer with you?" I walked up the stairs, closer to Rose.

"This is what I mean," Aine said. "Were I a lesser queen, such a tone from a monster would be a declaration of war."

"Chelle," Rose said, swallowing. "You should go."

"But—"

"I will talk to you later."

"I—"

Rose exhaled loudly. "That will be all."

She was making the biggest mistake of her life, but I couldn't force the issue in front of Queen Aine. Instead, I gripped the black key in my hand and spun away with a glare. I had to get out of the castle and recover the book as quickly as possible and hope against hope that Rose would unlock its secrets and come home with me.

And that she wouldn't hate me too much for abandoning her. I took one last look at the two queens and could have sworn I saw a smirk across Queen Aine's tiny face. I wanted so badly to end her, but she had given me my first lead in weeks, and I had to give her credit for that.

CHAPTER 4

RED

"How confident are you that Queen Aine is telling the truth?" I asked Chelle after she finished debriefing me about her meeting with the Unseelie queen. I'd had run-ins with Queen Aine many times before in my centuries in Urgu, and I took everything she said with a grain of salt and a pinch of distrust.

"Twenty percent, give or take," she replied.

I had just returned from a scouting mission to Critterton, because my intel told me the Wicked Witch had been spotted, but my trip proved fruitless. Though I liked being away from the castle, it pained me to keep missing on Nimue, following dead end trails.

"That's not very much," I said with a rueful sigh.

"It's not, but it would explain why nobody saw her leave the kingdom, either by flight or by crossing the Gates of Droangor."

The Gates of Droangor were the only point of entry through the Wall of Itherium which protected Hypnos's kingdom from the others in Urgu. It was guarded by a battalion of soldiers and dozens of magical wards that had prevented it from being breeched for over two thousand years.

The Gates sat at the edge of Hypnos's border with Hera's Dark Domain. Hypnos took no great pleasure in walling himself off from the rest of the kingdoms, but it was necessary, given his disappearance, to keep his people safe and the Land of Oz protected from invasion. If only he could have predicted subterfuge by the likes of Nimue and Hera, perhaps he would still be with us today.

"We should put together a squadron and set out at once," I said.

Chelle shook her head. "I don't want to take any more troops from Rose's protection than absolutely necessary. I think we need to go alone."

I considered this. "Very well. We'll move faster that way, but are you sure you want to come with me? Rose still hasn't learned how to use her powers. She's in a very dangerous place right now. She could use all the allies she can find."

Chelle gritted her teeth. "It's specifically because she doesn't know what she's doing that I need to act fast. There's still time to get her away from this foolish idea that she should stay in the Dream Realm. The longer she stays, the more she'll fall under the spell of this place. If she learns how to use her powers, and how to be queen, I fear she'll never come home."

Personally, I was bitter that Rose chose to stay in Urgu over returning to Earth. I would give everything to leave the waking nightmare of the Dream Realm behind. Yes, Urgu brought unnaturally long life, but no one should live forever. A finite lifespan was intimately tied to humanity, and the longer I lived, the further I felt from my mortality, and even what it felt to feel.

Earth.

Honestly, I could barely remember it, and if I could remember it, I didn't know if it was a real memory, or just an illusion I created over my long years in Urgu. *Was I really ever so young as my memories, or have I always been this fully-grown person, clad in a red cape, that I see when I look in a mirror?*

"You make a point." I nodded. "If there is any chance to save your paramour's soul, then we must make haste. I will speak to Balor. If he is rested enough, he will make a fine protector for our queen."

"Thank you."

I made my way to the armory, where I found Balor rocking in a chair in the corner, watching the dwarves make weaponry for the Queen's Guard. There were no more powerful hands for making weapons than the dwarves, but most of them were in the mines collecting dreams to fill Oz's coffers. Those that worked in the armory were the best of the best.

"Gtho!" Balor shouted, picking up a broadsword lying next to him. "This hilt needs to be restrung with a new leather grip. It will slip from our men's hands otherwise."

Balor spun the sword around and handed it to a small dwarf with beady eyes and a long red beard. They could have been brothers. Balor would be the elder, of course, for he was fully grown, but still stocky and packed with muscle, sporting the same full, bushy red beard.

"What ho, good Balor!" I called to him, pushing back my long cape as he stood and wrapped me in a hug.

"Belle, you beautiful thing, you," he said, spinning me around. "What are you doing down in the dregs of the castle?"

"I come to call on you, my friend. How do you feel?"

Balor cracked his neck to one side, then the other. "Better, I reckon. There's not a garrison of men who could take me on." Even as he spoke the words, he slumped down to the ground, his face contorted in pain.

"Are you sure, my friend?" I asked. "You don't look well."

Balor had nearly been killed in the riots following the death of Queen Ozma just a few weeks earlier. He was protecting our rear flank while Chelle and I disappeared into the castle to rescue Rose, and Nimue's troops descended upon him. I thought it would be the last time I saw him alive, but he survived—partially because of his legendary fighting prowess, partially because he had the ability to turn himself into a cyclops and wreak havoc on the Queen's Guard, and partially because after the death of Ozma, the denizens of Oz stormed the castle and fought the Queen's Guard themselves, giving us a chance to finish our mission, save Rose, and banish Nimue.

Balor became a hero to the townsfolk after the legendary battle, but the attack scuffed him up considerably, and he had been on the mend for weeks.

"I'm fine," he said, limping towards his rocking chair with a loud huff.

"That is good, because I have a favor to ask of you," I said.

"Aye, of course you do, lass. That is your way. What is it?"

I took a step closer to him. "Chelle got intel from Queen Aine that Nimue is in the Dark Domain, hiding out at Hera's castle."

"And you believe the fairy? She's the queen of all lies."

"It's a hierarchy of distrust, Balor. Hera is the worst of them, then Nimue, then Aine, and right now, one is telling tales about the other. I don't want to believe, but I also have no other leads from as high a source. We must find Nimue before she devises another plot and attacks us before we're ready."

Balor winced, easing into his chair. "Do you think it's possible?"

I nodded. "I think anything is possible when it comes to the Wicked Witch."

"But the Gates of Droangor are meant to hold back any attack. Surely—"

"And yet, Nimue escaped through them. She was queen for a hundred years. She didn't keep her crown due to her people's love for her. She is cunning and crafty. She will be back, that much I know. Her thirst for power is insidious and insatiable."

"You must follow your gut. It has never led you astray before."

Balor was right. My gut instinct was the stuff of legend. Years ago, when I met the fates and learned my body had died on Earth, I asked them to make me useful to Hypnos. In doing so, they gave me legendary instincts, which have kept me from dying, and always pointed me toward the north star. I have not always found the light, but my gut had kept me alive, and it brought me to Rose. Now, it was telling me that I had to get to Hera's kingdom quickly, before Nimue and Hera formulated a plan of attack.

"Then you will help me?"

Balor nodded. "Of course. I shall protect the queen as if she were you, whom I love more than I did my own kin."

I smiled. "That's not saying much. To have you tell it, your kin were not very nice."

Balor attempted to stand, then collapsed back into his

chair. "No, they were not, and yet I loved them like no other, save you."

I held up my finger. "Don't get sappy on me now, Balor. It's unbecoming."

He smiled. "Sorry, my lady."

"And please don't call me that ever again."

I feared that Balor would not be able to carry out his duties as protector, but I had no other choice. There was none other in the castle whom I trusted, and the rest of Ozma's forces had scattered to the wind.

CHAPTER 5

CHELLE

I wasn't confident that Balor's broken body could protect Rose. I knew who could, given the right incentive, but it meant pleading with an old enemy for help.

I didn't like to grovel.

No. That wasn't a strong enough sentiment. I HATED groveling.

I certainly didn't want to grovel to one of my least favorite people in all of Urgu. However, if I wanted to make sure that Rose was safe, I knew the best chance, aside from Balor who still needed time to mend, was to make a deal with Queen Aine, the person most likely working with the Wicked Witch to recapture the throne.

Rose put her up in the East Tower, the grandest, most luxurious place in the whole of the Emerald City. I climbed the stairs to the top of the tower, where I was confronted with four hovering bulbs of light. From my previous inter-action with the fae, I knew this was their way, to hover invisibly with only their glow showing, until they were forced to reveal themselves.

"Halt! Intruder!" The silver ball of light transfigured

into one of Queen Aine's palanquin bearers. "You are not authorized to come any closer to the fairy queen."

I sighed and pinched the bridge of my nose. The sound of their high-pitched voices gave me a headache. "Can you just tell the queen that I am here to see her?"

"And who are you?" Another ball of light said. "Besides a disgusting monster."

I bit the side of my cheek to prevent myself from lashing out at them. "Chelle. The gorgon. I'm sure she will remember me."

"Think very highly of yourself, don't you?" A third ball of light said. "As if our queen has time to deal with the likes of you, or even to remember something so...hideous as you are is laughable."

"I'm not here to argue. I'm just here to see the queen. Please, don't make me fight you. This will be so much easier if you just let me through."

"I'm afraid we can't do that," the first ball of light said.

"I figured as much," I replied, sighing. "*Flammis venit ad me.*" My hands filled with orange flame. The heat felt good in my hands, and I couldn't help but smirk as I looked up at the fairies. "Last chance."

The other guards revealed themselves. All four of them vibrated violently until a flash of light filled the room. I blocked my eyes for a moment, and then when the light was gone, I pushed the fire from my hands toward the fae guards.

The fae dodged my attack and charged together. I ducked beneath them and then bounded up the staircase, with a clear pathway up the stairs to Queen Aine's bedchamber.

"*Obice glacies praesidium!*" I shouted and a wall of ice poured out of my arms, coating the hallway. The guards tried to stop, but they merely rammed into the ice wall. They reared back and attacked again. This time the ice buckled, and then with a second charge it broke, but that was fine with me. I was just buying time.

I closed my eyes and when I opened them, they were orange. "Listen to me," I hissed with a snakelike voice. The four fae stopped in their tracks. "Stand down, all of you, and forget you saw me. Understood?"

Hypnosis was the most powerful and dangerous of my powers, and the only one I could do without a spell, as it came as a natural gift from my gorgon mother. However, it drained my energy faster than anything, which meant I couldn't hold them for long.

"Understood," the fae guards said in unison.

"Good." I turned away and ran up the stairs until I reached the large wooden door at the top of the cylindrical staircase.

"*Flammis venit ad me!*" I shouted, and my hands lit up again with flames.

"Please. None of that," Queen Aine said from behind her chamber door. She snapped her fingers and the door opened. "If you're going to come in, please put your glowing eyes away, too."

I blinked and took a deep breath, my eyes turning back to their normal green and the fire leaving my hands. It was my first time at the East Tower, but I had heard that it was a favorite of the fairy queen's. Decorated in purple, the bed was small enough that it made her feel welcome, but large enough that it didn't make her feel condescended to by a castle of larger people.

Queen Aine sat against the window, looking out at the mountains. "Hera's castle can be seen even here. It's a far way off, and you have a long way to go. Yet, you are still here. Why?"

"I don't believe you."

"And you shouldn't. However, please know that I could have you hanged for your treason just now and declare war on all of Oz for your insolence. You clearly love your queen, but you are impetuous and don't think about the consequences of your actions."

I chuckled. "I can't argue with that."

"Of course you can't," Queen Aine scoffed. "I'm a queen. Nobody dares argue with a queen."

I shrugged. "I argue with Rose all the time."

Queen Aine rolled her eyes. "Yes, I can tell. No wonder why she is so meek and frail."

"Hey! I protect her, too."

"Even worse. A queen needs to exude power out of every pore. She is one of the most powerful, perhaps the most powerful, being in all of Urgu, and she carries herself like a child."

"I know," I said after a long pause. "I'm trying, but no matter what I do, I just seem to make it worse."

"Of course you do," Queen Aine said. "She needs lessons on being a queen from an *actual* queen. You have a habit of killing them off or driving them away."

"Except for you, is that the implication?" I wasn't stupid, but it's important to be clear when dealing with the fae. "That she should learn from you?"

Queen Aine turned to me. "Oh, gods no. I simply don't have either the *time* or the *inclination*."

I raised an eyebrow, so she knew I didn't believe her.

She sighed. "I will advise her until the coronation, but I don't have the energy for a top-to-bottom overhaul, which is what it would take to make your Rose queen-worthy."

"Enough of this circuitous bullshit. You clearly know why I'm here."

A sly smile spread across Queen Aine's face. "Why, whatever do you mean?"

"I need your help." I took a long moment. "Rose needs your help. I'm going to Hera's castle. While I'm gone, somebody has to look after her."

"And you want me to do it? Surely there are bodyguards for that kind of thing."

"She has protection, but you know as well as I do that the Queen's Guard can't be trusted. Half are still loyal to Nimue, and we don't know which half. Until we know who's conspiring against us, I can't trust anybody."

"And you trust me?"

"No. But I will make a deal with you. If you agree to a deal, you are bound to it, are you not?"

"I am." The fairy queen nodded. "That is the fairy code."

I sighed. "Then protect Rose until I return, and I will do anything you wish."

"I have already pledged allegiance to her."

"That is a weak bond, which can be broken. I want to make a deal which you can't wriggle out of so easily."

A smirk appeared on her face. "You would make a deal with a fairy, even knowing how we work to break them and twist them?"

"Yes, because I know you also can't break a pact, no matter what, without losing your powers permanently. If I speak simply, then I can save Rose."

"And what of you? You will be bound to our deal as well."

"I don't care what happens to me."

Aine laughed. "I overestimated your cleverness. You really are dumb."

I shook my head. "Not dumb. Just in love."

"Same thing." Her disgust attached itself to every word. "Very well, I will take your deal. I will protect Rose until you return, and in exchange...I simply ask for your wish to the fates."

I wasn't expecting that to be her part of the deal. I needed that wish to get Rose home in case she wouldn't come with me willingly. "I can't...what if..."

"Can't or won't?"

"I...what if Rose won't go with me willingly?"

"Then you will force her? That is not very loving."

I sighed. "I will. She is seduced by this place, but it is not what's best for her."

Queen Aine cackled loudly. "I love it. I absolutely love it. You would betray the one you claim to love. That is too wonderful. Okay, then. I will let you keep your wish. However, I would ask something else."

"Anything."

"A favor of my choice, to be used when I choose to use it."

I took a deep breath. I knew I was being tricked, but Queen Aine knew this world better than me, and her magic was more powerful. I just had to hope when the time came, I would be able to protect myself. "As long as it doesn't hurt Rose."

Queen Aine nodded. "Fair enough. I swear it will not hurt Rose."

"And you will not hurt Rose."

"And I will not hurt Rose."

"And you will do everything in your power to keep her safe until my return."

"...until your return."

I nodded and held out my hand. "Then it is a deal."

Every bone in my body told me I was making a mistake, but I didn't care. It was the only way I could think to keep Rose safe.

Queen Aine floated over to me and placed her hand on mine. Her hands glowed purple, and once we touched, the glow covered my whole hand as well, and then the rest of my body along with hers. It was warm and cool all at once, and then, as soon as the light had come, it disappeared.

"Then our pact is sealed."

CHAPTER 6

ROSE

"What are you talking about? You're leaving?" I glared hard at Chelle as she sat on the couch across from my bed. "You can't leave!"

I hated my bedchamber. Like the rest of the castle, it still had all of Nimue's accoutrements, down to the creepy mirror which spun around all day every day as if it were being drained like a toilet. It was filled with macabre paintings and sculptures that made me jump every time I turned around. Nimue had horrible taste. Even the bed was covered with black silk sheets and topped with black wrought iron and twisted demons cackling along the headboard.

Dark curtains prevented any light from entering from outside, so the only light in the room came from the spiraling mirror along the far wall, and candles placed strategically around the room. They barely prevented me from tripping over everything, even in the bright light of day.

"Well, that's weird, because I'm leaving," Chelle replied,

dispassionately, as if she didn't care at all that she was breaking my heart.

I shuddered, trying to formulate my thoughts. "There are all sorts of people who can do that. I have, like, a whole army of people now, Chelle. You don't need to go."

"Nimue's still out there, Rose. And I have to find the book."

That book. That stupid book. Another way to open the Obsidian Spindle and go home. I didn't want to go home. I prayed against hope that Chelle would forget about leaving the Dream Realm and just be happy we were together, but no matter how much I tried to give her everything, she couldn't be happy here. I thought I was enough for her.

"I know you don't want me to go," Chelle said in a low voice.

"It's not that," I replied with a deep sigh. "I just want you to be happy...with me. I want you to be happy here because I'm happy."

Chelle shook her head. "I don't believe you're happy."

"Why?" I threw up my hands. "Why can't you believe that I know what I want?"

"Because look around you, Rose!" Chelle shouted, pushing up from her chair. "Not one person we've met here is happy. Any one of them would kill to have what we have."

My voice rose to match the indignity of her tone. "A loving relationship?"

"Bodies, baby," Chelle said with a smile.

"You're mistaken." I shook my head. "I don't have a body. I came here through my dreams just like everybody else. You're the only one with a body in the Dream Realm."

Every other being in The Dream Realm had entered either

through their dreams or through the imagination of a dreamer. Not Chelle, though. She came through a door guarded by Mydnyte, a devotee of Nox, the goddess of Darkness and the Night. She walked in with her body intact, because of course she did. She never did anything the normal way, not that anything was normal about this whole situation. The bottom line was that she had what nobody else in Urgu had: a body. Many believed that meant she could manipulate the hand of fate like none other in the Dream Realm.

"You don't have a body here," Chelle replied. "But you have one waiting for you back on Earth, which is more than literally anybody else can say in all of Urgu." Chelle walked over and sat down next to me. "The Wicked Witch, the Fairy Queen, Red, Balor, even Hera would literally kill to get access to a body. These are some of the most powerful people in all of Urgu, and all they want is to go back to Earth, so they can be nothing burgers."

She was right. My body was lying in a hospital bed in a diabetic coma, wasting away with each passing moment... but it was there, just waiting for me to return so I could wake up.

Chelle tried to place her hands on mine, but I pulled them away. "I've been a nothing burger my whole life. This is better."

"Even if you think it's better, what will you think in a hundred years, or a thousand, or even tomorrow? Not one person I've talked to hasn't missed their body something fierce, and you have a chance to get yours back."

"I don't want it."

"And what about me?" Chelle said, lowering her eyes.

"What about you?"

"I still have my body, Rose. What happens when it starts to give out? What happens when it dies?"

I hadn't thought about that. Chelle looked the same as every other person in Urgu, but she wasn't. She was a singular being with a body in a place where no one had a body.

"We'll figure that out," I said, swallowing, "when the time comes."

Chelle stood up. "I don't want to figure it out when the time comes, Rose. I want to get out of here, and I want you to come with me."

I turned from her, not wanting her to see the tears in my eyes. "I'm not going to stop you from leaving, Chelle. And if you bring that book back, and I can read it, I'll help you open the Spindle, but I'm not going back. Do you hear me?"

Chelle nodded. "I hear you. I don't agree with you, but I hear you."

"And if you leave, there's no guarantee that you'll come back...ever. I was the first dreamer to enter Urgu in a century, remember?"

Chelle smiled. "I'm pretty stubborn. I'll find a way."

I chuckled despite myself. "That, I believe." I turned back to Chelle and wiped the tears from my eyes. "What am I going to do without you here? You're supposed to protect me."

Chelle avoided eye contact. She was embarrassed, ashamed about something, and she bit her lip to avoid telling me.

"What aren't you saying?"

"Nothing," she muttered.

"Don't lie to me. I'm your girlfriend, and your queen."

She sighed. "I've made a deal for your protection, with Queen Aine."

I leapt up from the bed. "The Unseelie Queen! How could you? Don't you know—"

"Of course I know the risks, but I also know these are dangerous times, and without me here, somebody with magical ability has to protect you, and somebody with queenly duties has to train you for your coronation. Queen Aine can do both."

I caught her eyes. "What did you promise her?"

Chelle looked away. "I...can't tell you."

I stood up straighter and pushed back my shoulders. "I demand you tell me. I am your queen."

She met my eyes, then. "That doesn't matter at all to me, and you know that. I couldn't tell you as my girlfriend, which is the most important thing in my life, but as my queen you must know, Queen Aine will protect you until I return."

"And what happens then?"

"Then, I will be here to protect you myself."

I raised my eyebrows. "Until you go through the Obsidian Spindle and return home."

Chelle's words fell out of her mouth aching with sadness. "Yes, until then."

I couldn't believe what I was hearing. "I think you should leave."

"I don't want to leave with you mad."

"Well, you pretty much guaranteed that when you made a deal with Queen Aine and decided to abscond in the night without my blessing."

"Please, Rose." Chelle clasped her hands together, begging. "I'm doing this for us. Can't you see that?"

"No, Chelle. You're doing this for you." I turned my back on her. "Guards! My guest was just leaving."

Two burly guards wearing uniforms embroidered with the white peacock of Hera walked into the room. "Yes, ma'am," one of them mumbled.

I faced them. "Please escort Chelle to the stables. Allow her to pick her horse, and make sure she leaves the castle safely."

"Yes, ma'am."

"And most importantly...Don't let her back inside to see me, no matter what, until she returns from her ridiculous quest."

"Yes, ma'am."

Tears welled in Chelle's eyes. "Please, don't do this. Don't let me leave like this."

I turned away from her once more as the guards grabbed her arms and pulled her away from me. I knew she could blow them apart with merely a thought, but she didn't, and she didn't say another word as they dragged her out of my sight and closed the door to my room.

The moment I was alone, I began to sob for the loss of my protector, for her betrayal, and for the love that I felt cracking in my chest, one I feared I would never be made whole again.

CHAPTER 7
NIMUE

Ow.

My head.

Where was I?

Ouch. My back hurts. *Why does my back hurt?*

Why is there a thorn in my butt?

A chill shot through me and the wind whipped across my stomach. I looked down to see my bare midriff, followed by my bare legs, and then my bare—*Wait, why was I naked?*

"Clothing," I said, waving my hands, but nothing happened. "Clothing!"

Again, nothing happened. I sighed, trying the Latin. "Fine. *Indumentis.*"

Still nothing. *"Indumentis."*

When the incantation still failed, I knew what had happened. Hera had revoked her blessing from me. I was all alone in the world. No blessing. No magic. Naked. I created my clothing with magic. Without magic, I had no clothing.

I looked up. The thatch of trees broke at their zenith and revealed Hera's mountain fortress, staring out from the rock. I was alone in the haunted woods below Hera's castle.

I didn't like the dark woods during the daylight with every ounce of my powers at my disposal, and now I liked them even less.

I had no choice but to traverse them alone until I found clothing and hopefully, some food to satiate my ravenous stomach. It had been over a thousand years since I'd experienced hunger, but I felt as though if I didn't eat soon, I would die and collapse into a million grains of dust, just like Ozma.

Ozma, the great scourge of my rule. I dropped her from the balcony of my castle and watched her explode into dust below me not a month ago. How my fortunes had changed since then.

The thought of her death brought a smile to my face, and I forgot my fate for a moment. It was a fate worse than death, to be alone in Urgu without the protection of the gods. No matter how petty and fickle she was, Hera had always protected me.

I had to learn to care for myself again or die trying. Of course, that was what Hera expected. She expected me to curl up in a ball and be eaten by the ravenous beasts roaming the woods. But I survived once without her magic, and I would do so again. She had no idea how strong I was, or how intense my will to live.

"Hurry!" I heard a voice shriek out in the darkness. I fell behind a tree to hide.

A group of people emerged into a clearing.

Or, they looked like people, though like few I had seen in my time in Urgu. Their light didn't pulsate like fairies, but kept a consistent, haunting glow. Their hair and eyes didn't flicker, either. The fairies I knew were vibrant, majestic, and beautiful, while these people looked more like colorful monsters lumbering through the woods.

A scientist had come into the Dream Realm shortly before the end of Hypnos's reign, and worked with me on developing several experiments to escape Urgu, before he disappointed me one too many times and I had no choice but to dust him. One of his experiments was based on a thing he had seen at an automobile show based on the capture of a gas inside of a tube.

He called it neon, and he spent years trying to perfect it for our purposes, but never got it to work properly. It was the closest thing I could think of to understanding what I saw in front of me. There was nothing else like this in all Urgu.

The bearers of the light walked through the night like they belonged there, as if it were bright as day, and I soon realized they must have been from the Argonian Mountains, where darkness never gave way to the morning. Even our bravest knights refused to travel up the mountains to meet with Agrona, fearing the devilry she developed in her mountains.

These were the Mountain People, sparse and nomadic, who moved at night. They rarely came to the Land of Oz, except for as refugees when the Mountains became too cruel for them.

"Move out!" the leader of the group said. Her hair was long and twisted into braids. Every strand glowed a different color, from blue to green and yellow to pink. It was hauntingly beautiful. "We can make it to the Gates of Droangor by morning if we don't let up."

The Gates. If I could get through them, I would be safe back inside Hypnos's kingdom. It was one thing to live in the Dark Domain, or the Bogs, or even the Sandlands without my magic. Even with my full arsenal it would have taken every ounce of cunning to survive, but now, without it, the only choice was to return to Hypnos's realm and try to build a life among the fairies, or stay hidden in the trees as a refugee.

I would have to infiltrate the group and find a way to join them without being spotted. I had no desire to be at their ghoulish mercy.

CHAPTER 8
CHELLE

"You can let go of me now," I said. The guards were true to the queen's command and led me out of the castle and all the way to the stables, each with a hand wrapped around my arm. I struggled against them, but not much.

The snakes atop my head did more to protest than I did. They lunged at the guards, even poor Albie with his missing tooth, until they bit into the metal of their armor and realized any attack hurt them more than it would hurt our abductors. After that, all they did was hiss and snap until the guards tossed me down and turned back to the castle without a word.

"That sucked," I said, standing up and brushing myself off. I wasn't surprised by the fact that Rose was angry with me. However, I was taken aback by the level of her anger, and how she used the power of her office to dispose of me like I was a rancid banana.

Perhaps it was best that we ended on such bad terms. It made it easy to do what I needed to do without the guilt of abandoning Rose. If we'd had a pleasant final meeting, it might have convinced me not to go, but the acrimony between us made my decision to leave much easier.

"Are you ready?" Red called. "Or are you going to keep causing a scene?"

"I'm sorry," I said, walking into the stables. Two beautiful black horses stood in front of me, with finely polished saddles and satchels hanging off either side of them.

Red pulled her red hood down. Her dark red lipstick accentuated her alabaster skin in the moonlight. "I don't know what we'll come into in the Dark Domain, so I packed us a variety of weapons, equipment, and potions just in case we run into something particularly nasty."

"Just in case?" I asked. "I thought that was guaranteed."

"I was being optimistic," Red replied, pulling herself onto her horse. "I meant when we do. It is better to be prepared than to need something and not have it."

I walked up to the horse Red had saddled for me. I wasn't comfortable riding horses, but I had taken to it a bit since coming to Urgu. There was no other way to move around, since I hadn't figured out a way to teleport by magic. It was either horses or walking.

"Thank you for taking the time to pack for me," I said.

"It wasn't a problem," Red said, adjusting the reigns on her steed. "I enjoy inventory, actually. My missions provide their own challenges but collecting and sorting inventory is...somewhat calming. It gives me a sense of control in a world that lacks it."

I hopped up onto my horse, grunting as I swung my leg over the saddle. There was a grace that Red had with horses that I just couldn't match. Of course, she had been riding horses for hundreds of years, and until I came to Urgu I had only done it once, on a very bad date back in high school.

"How did Rose take it?" Red asked.

I sighed. "Badly, as you would expect."

"She will understand when you come back with the book, I hope?"

"Will she?" I wondered out loud. "She doesn't seem to want to leave this place, even though it's crazy to stay. I mean, right? She has a perfectly good body waiting on Earth!"

"I believe it would be a slap in the face of every resident in Urgu to stay here when you have a perfectly good body waiting for you on Earth."

"Thank you! That's what I've been trying to tell her but being queen has made her thick headed."

Red looked at me over her shoulder. "I'm sure you will be able to talk some sense into her eventually. After all, you are quite stubborn yourself."

I smiled. "I'll take that as a compliment."

"Perhaps a backhanded compliment." Red kicked her stirrups and her horse trotted out of the stable.

I brushed the mane of my horse and leaned down to its ear. "Just take it slow, okay? I'm not good at riding, okay?"

The horse whinnied back.

"What is your name?" I asked, still stroking its mane.

"She's not a magical horse, just a normal one without vocal cords," Red said from the stable entrance. "Her name is Biscuit."

"That's a stupid name," I replied. Then I looked down at the horse, who seemed to turn away from me, indignant. "Sorry. Let's just go."

I clicked my stirrups and the horse trotted out of the stable. As I neared Red and her horse, two lights flickered at the entrance to the castle. A small purple bulb trailed the orange light of a candle across the courtyard. When it closed on me, I could make out Rose, lit by candlelight, wearing a white nightgown, and clutching her free fist to her chest. The purple orb floated around her head.

Red bowed her head. "My lady."

Rose nodded to her. "If you don't mind, I would like to talk to my girlfriend."

"Of course." Red and her horse trotted out of the way.

Rose walked through the rest of the courtyard to me. Her face was cold, but her eyes were filled with grief and sadness.

"Hi," I said, trying to take a measure of the conversation.

"I don't like how we ended things," Rose said.

"Me either."

"I don't like what you're doing, but if this is the last time we see each other, we shouldn't leave angry."

I frowned. "Don't even talk like that."

"I'm the queen," she replied with a sad smile. "I can talk any way I want."

"Fair enough, but I will be back, and you will be queen, and then, we will go home."

Rose sighed. "We'll talk about that when you get back —if you come back—but you are right. This will not be the last time I see you." She unclasped her hand and in it was a small locket.

"Wear this. Queen Aine enchanted it so that it connects with the mirror in my room. When you look into it, you will see me. We will be connected."

"What if Hera is watching, too?" I said. "After all, that mirror is hers."

"Let her watch me."

"And what if she's watching through the necklace?"

Queen Aine materialized from the purple orb near Rose. "She won't."

"How do you know?"

"I am a very good enchantress. The rival to any on Earth or in Urgu."

I bent down and took the necklace from Rose's outstretched hand. As I did, my fingers brushed hers, and my heart skipped a beat. I took the necklace and placed it around my neck.

"I will keep it with me at all times."

"See that you do. Otherwise, my heart with break in half."

"I'm sorry—Ro—"

"No, you're not," Rose said. "Don't lie to me. Not now."

I nodded, gripping the locket. "I will come back."

Rose tried to smile, but she couldn't. Instead, she turned and fled back to the castle, leaving Queen Aine behind. The fairy queen handed me a small note.

"Bring this note to my captain at the entrance to the Enchanted Woods, and Muirgen will take you to the Gates of Droangor. It will take a week off your trip."

"Why are you helping me?"

"The sooner you get back, the sooner I can be relieved of my duty to your very whiny girlfriend."

"You'll grow to love her," I said.

"No, I won't. Of that I assure you."

"Trust me. You will. She's very loveable."

"Unlike her girlfriend," Red had circled back around and butted into the conversation with a wry smile. "Queen Aine, please tell Rose that Balor will be her personal body-guard when he is mended, which I hope will be on the morrow."

"I'm not a courier," Queen Aine replied.

"I know," Red said, dipping her head. "It would be a great favor to me as I was unable to tell her before she left."

"Very well," Queen Aine said. "I will relay the message, but only because I know your low birth and raising leads you to mean no offense by your insult."

With that, the fairy queen fluttered toward the castle.

"I hate her so much," Red said.

"Ditto," I replied. "Come on. Let's go."

CHAPTER 9
ROSE

I couldn't show any amount of weakness as I watched Chelle and Red ride through the gates and off into the darkness, but my heart tore with each stride she took away from me. I bit my lip and reentered the castle.

"It will never be easier," Queen Aine said, floating after me. "You can harden to it, though. I have sent my share of brave soldiers off to war and watched as only a handful of them returned. Once, a fairy I loved more than any other led the charge against my bitter rival, and never returned. That was a hard day. There are many hard days."

"But I did not send her away," I replied as the door closed behind me. "In fact, quite the opposite, I begged her to stay."

"That is because you lack the gravitas of a queen."

I cocked my head, frowning. "But I am a queen."

"No," Queen Aine replied in a low voice. "You have the title, or will once the coronation ceremony has completed, but you do not have the posture, voice, or power of a queen. Even if I were to lose everything tomorrow, my power would remain. I have learned what needed to be done to always be a queen, no matter the circumstance. It is precisely my power which keeps my power."

I didn't fully understand her words, but I knew she was right. Perhaps one day, with her help, I could project the same power she conveyed so effortlessly. I could only hope. "Thank you."

I followed two guards through the winding hallways toward my bed chamber. The hallways were nothing like the throne room, or my bed chamber, and they filled me with whimsy. It felt like a proper castle here, and not a haunted gothic mansion. These walls were decorated with colorful, hand-painted flowers. Candles lined the hallways, and paintings of the queens that came before looked down upon me as I walked through. I still couldn't help staring at the high ceilings covered in reliefs of the gods and monsters of legend. I knew those legends had much truth to them.

"You will learn it all in time," Aine said.

I squeezed my head with my palms. "Maybe, but all this queening makes my head hurt."

"Don't do that with your hands. It is unbecoming."

I placed my hands at my sides. "I'm sorry. Wait, why did I do that?"

"Because I commanded it."

"Are you controlling my mind?" I asked.

Queen Aine shook her head. "No, my dear. I don't have to control you in that way. I control you with my voice, and with my power, which emanates from me always."

"And you can teach this to me?"

"I will do my best."

"FOR THE TRUE QUEEN!" a loud voice shouted as we turned the corner. Something scampered down the hall toward me. I heard the patter of feet but all I saw was the flash of purple light as something exploded. I fell to the floor.

It was over in a moment. My ears rang as I pushed myself to my knees, squinting through the black smoke. Queen Aine materialized a purple forcefield around us both. Dust rose into the air and mixed with black soot.

All of my guards were dusted. It was just me and Queen Aine now. The paintings I'd been admiring moments before had shattered, the perfectly accented walls around us collapsed in the explosion.

"What happened?" I asked, panting.

"There was just an attempt on your life, dear. First time?"

I nodded, still out of breath. "Since becoming queen, at least. You did try to kill me once, after all."

Aine ignored my comment. "This may have been the first time, but it won't be that last. We have a lot of work to do. I fear nowhere in this palace is safe."

I agreed with her. The only two people I trusted in all of Urgu were now gone, and I was on my own with only one of my oldest enemies for protection, and the hope that the deal Chelle struck would be enough to keep me safe until she returned.

CHAPTER 10

RED

"I don't get it," I said to Chelle once we were out of Oz and on the road to K'Dech. It was the last town on the Queen's Road before reaching the Enchanted Woods, and an infamous stop for wayward travelers on their way through the Land of Oz.

"What don't you get?" Chelle asked. She was trying desperately to stay on her horse. Hours of training lessons since she became the queen's paramour did little for her coordination. She clung on for dear life.

"I understand what you see in Rose. She's nice, and sweet, and way too good for you."

"Thank you. I'm still waiting for a question, though."

"What does she see in you?" I asked. I didn't need to be coy about it. Chelle and I did not have that kind of relationship.

Chelle, to her credit, laughed, instead of snarling at me. Either option was equally likely, and equally appropriate. "I don't know, honestly. I've always been surly and guarded, and Rose never cared at all. Has she ever told you about her high school boyfriend?"

I wasn't sure exactly what she meant by high school. We barely had any type of school while I was on Earth, high, low, or otherwise. "No. She has not told me about high school at all. What is a high school?"

Chelle rolled her eyes. "Right. You're old. They probably didn't have school in your time."

"I am aware of school. Maybe people have told me about going to school in my travels, but they did not delineate high school from low school."

Chelle chuckled again. "It's not called high school or low school. There's elementary school. Then middle school. Then high school. Then college. Well, there could be junior high in there as well, but not where I lived."

"How many years of schooling is that?"

"I guess if you count kindergarten and preschool, and assume you graduate college, something like twenty?"

"Twenty years in school? In my day, you would have three children and likely be close to death by the age of twenty. What do you learn in this high school?"

"Gods, that is another good question. It seems like nothing, most of the time."

"And Rose, she had a boyfriend in this thing you call high school, despite having you as a girlfriend now?"

"Yup," Chelle nodded. "She was a bit...confused when we met."

"What's to say she isn't confused now?"

Chelle looked to the sky for a moment, deep in thought. "Nothing, I guess."

"Now I'm confused."

Chelle shrugged. "Yeah, well, welcome to my life. That's what it's like to grow up in the twenty-first century."

I wanted to get our conversation back on track. "I assume this boyfriend was not very nice."

Chelle scrunched up her face, like she just tasted a bitter root, and shook her head. "No, he wasn't very nice. He was physically and emotionally abusive. He used her for her body, and even though she told her parents about it, they still loved him. That's the worst part. He treated her horribly, but he was a boy, so they loved him. Me, they hate…"

"Because you are a girl."

"A black girl."

I scoffed. "That's crazy."

"Thank—"

"You are clearly a gorgon. If anything, they should hate you for that reason."

Chelle laughed again, making a face. "Yeah, well they definitely don't know about that."

"Ah, and they would hate you more if they knew that?"

"Hate me? No, they would probably kill me if they knew. It's not legal to kill a black person, even in the deepest and most racist parts of the Klan country, but killing a gorgon, there's no legal precedent for that. Deaths of monsters usually falls under the 'don't ask, don't tell' part of the law."

In my life, people believed in monsters, and gods, and fairy tales. It surprised me to learn people now felt otherwise. "So, people on Earth no longer believe in monsters?" I asked.

"Not really."

"And what about pictures? Do people not see pictures of monsters all the time?"

"Yeah, but people just figure the photographer used filters, or photoshopped them. Nobody believes anything these days. We have a problem with objective truth."

"I don't fully understand what you're talking about, but

I do understand about nobody believing or wanting to believe. In my time, we had the opposite problem. Humans wanted so badly to believe they were the most advanced life on Earth, and would do anything to hold that belief, no matter who they hurt doing it."

"In that way, people haven't changed much in hundreds of years."

There was a long silence. The only thing that we heard was the clomping of horse feet and the jingling of saddles. The air whipped across our faces, and the smell of flowers filled my nose.

"If humans hate monsters so much, then why does Rose like you?"

Chelle sighed. "I was hoping you forgot about that question."

"I did not."

"People aren't nice to Rose very often. Her parents, her exes, even her friends treated her like garbage for a long time. I don't."

"Ah, I see. So because you treat her slightly better than the others, she sees you as some sort of hero?"

"Slightly better?" Chelle scoffed. "Bitch, please. I treat her like a goddess."

"That is not a compliment, in these parts."

"Point taken."

"I'm just saying, you fully intend to bring Rose back to Earth against her wishes. That doesn't seem to be taking her opinion into account or doing what is best for her."

"It is what's best for her. She just doesn't know it. Rose doesn't know what she wants. Being here is easy. She's somebody here, and she thinks she'll be a nobody on Earth, but she's not a nobody. She matters a lot, to me."

"And you think that should be enough for her?"

"Can we change the subject? Why don't you tell me where we're going after K'dech?"

I sighed. I had no interest in discussing such trivial matters, but I humored her. "Well, you remember the way, I assume, back through the Enchanted Woods, past Critterton, and then—"

"And then I don't know what is south of Critterton."

"The furthest point south of Hypnos's kingdom, the Gates of Droagamir."

"I read about them. They are the only passage from the Land of Oz into the rest of Urgu. They sit at the border of the Dark Domain, where Hera is...but why build a wall around the kingdom, if Hera can just fly over?"

"Because Hera cannot bring an army through the gates into Oz. She has limits to her power, tamped down by runes carved into the Wall of Itherium, which surrounds the kingdom on all sides. It's the greatest barrier in all of Urgu. It keeps us safe, even after one hundred years of Queen Nimue's rule, and all those wars between the gods."

"Which land is the most dangerous?"

It was a worthy question. "They are all bad. The Sandlands, controlled by Sehkmet, have the most poisonous creatures you will ever run across. The sun scorches you through the forbidden deserts and awful creatures pop out of the sand out of nowhere. Loki's Boglands are filled with nasty swamps and huge, slimy monsters. The people of the Boglands are not gracious to visitors, which runs all the way to their king, who would sooner dust you than meet with you. Hera keeps the darkest creatures in her forests to prevent any from coming close. It is a haven for the dark arts, where necromancers and shadow creatures wait to take unsuspecting lots to their doom."

"Glad we're going there, then," Chelle snickered.

"Nowhere is safe outside of Oz," I replied. "The Mistreach is an eternal fog that Anansi's people use to cavort in secret. The mist plays tricks on the eyes. You will lose your mind if you don't know your way. But if I must choose, then the Mountains—that is the worst place of them all."

"Why?"

I swallowed. The things I had seen in the mountains, I could not unsee, or properly explain. "I don't know what Agrona is doing in those mountains, but it is evil on a scale even Hera cannot imagine."

"That sounds foreboding, but like, can you give me an example?"

I racked my brain, trying to come up with a description of the creatures I had seen there, but every time I flashed on one, my brain froze, and my head pounded. I felt my face twist and contort until I nearly fell off my steed. Chelle had to catch me by the shoulder and steady me.

"I'm sorry," she said, clearly sensing my reticence. "I shouldn't have—"

"No, it's okay. I have asked you far worse this day. It's just...I cannot fathom that which dwells in the mountains of Agrona's kingdom."

"Fair enough." Chelle turned away. "Maybe we can just be quiet for a while."

"Yes, of course. You always like to chatter on, so I was indulging you, but if you prefer to ride in silence, that's fine with me."

"Perfect."

"K'dech is just over the third ridge. We should get there by daylight if we hurry."

Chelle snapped the reins of her horse. "Then let's hurry."

CHAPTER II
CHELLE

We rode in silence most of the way to K'dech. The town was little more than a few ramshackle cottages, especially after the destruction of the Happy Dragon Inn several weeks before, but Red insisted we stop and rest. She and I had become quite a bit more familiar since Ozma died, but sometimes, she was difficult to deal with.

I took it to be because she was out in the wilderness, by herself for long stretches, and didn't know how to speak with people appropriately, but I resented her constant questions, and the way she spoke her mind without a second thought. There were some things I didn't even like talking about with Rose, and I certainly didn't like talking about them with somebody I hardly knew.

Once we turned into town, I suddenly understood why we had returned to K'Dech. In the middle of town sat a newly constructed and lively Happy Dragon Inn. The music filled the streets and warmed my heart even from a hundred yards away. There was no other reason to enter K'Dech except for the Happy Dragon.

"It's back," I said with a smile.

"Sure is," Red replied, dismounting. "You have never been here, and I think of it so fondly. I thought you should see it for yourself."

A dragon had burnt the Happy Dragon Inn, along with all its occupants, save the owner, an orc named Sam'il, during Rose and my initial days in Urgu. It was said to be protected by Hypnos himself, and when his power faded, so did his ability to protect the inn.

"How—"

Red was petting her horse and not looking at me. "I don't know. One day it was burnt and destroyed, the land salted so it could never return, and the next time I passed through the town to pay my respects, the inn stood as if it never left. Perhaps, the return of Hypnos, even for a moment to bestow his blessing on Rose, brought magic back to the inn, and allowed it to stand resurrected."

"Or maybe, Sam'il worked hard to build it back from scratch." I hopped down from my horse and tied its reins to the hitching post across from the inn. If the dragon returned, we didn't want to risk our horses being burned in the fire fight.

"I've known Sam'il for many years, and he is not one to work hard at anything. Now come. Let us celebrate the return of my favorite bar in Oz."

"Shouldn't we be going, though?" I said. "We have a job to do."

"We have been on the road for twelve hours. I'm tired of the road, aren't you?"

I nodded. My body ached for rest. The weariness was worse for me than others in Urgu. They didn't have to sleep. I still had a body, and that included all the trappings associated with one. Even Red felt the effects, though she rarely acted on it. She once told me a story of foregoing sleep, food, and drink for weeks, and while she was no worse for wear physically, her mind took months to recover.

I followed Red through the wooden door to the inn festooned with happy, fat, little, chibi dragons. The room was rowdy and loud, filled with nasty looking men and women. Each had seen their share of battle, and now drank themselves stupid in the bar. I had never been inside before, but Red talked about it often enough that it seemed familiar to me as well.

The last time I was here, when the inn was already burnt, I thought Rose had been inside. She had escaped, but unlucky for me, the Wicked Witch was at the site, and captured both me and my friend Diedre. Deidre had been disgusted to discover I was a monster, but she didn't deserve the death she was dealt, murdered by the Nimue in her throne room. It gave me all the more reason to stick a knife through the Wicked Witch's body.

"This is the most popular watering hole in all of Oz," Red said, walking up to the bar. "No matter how barren and bleak everything looks around it, this place is always packed. Legend has it that at the beginning of the Dream Realm, this was where Hypnos drank, before his duties as jailer to the gods pulled him away."

A halfling with one eye and pocked cheeks laughed heartily and threw his head back, falling into me. I pushed him back with his friends and spun around to Red who was already making her way to the bar.

"Sam'il!" Red said with a smile.

The green orc had long, gnarled, pointy ears and one of his yellow eyes was permanently closed shut. He wore a tattered apron around himself, covered with sauces, sweat, and blood. "Why, if it isn't Red?" he said with a lopsided smile. Several of his nasty, yellow teeth were missing. "I thought you'd forgotten about us."

"Forgotten? I didn't know you still existed. Last time I saw this place, it was being burned by a dragon."

Everything stopped. The air left the room as all eyes turned to Red.

"Don't worry, fellas," Sam'il said. "We're just havin' a friendly chat."

"What's the rule?" a bulbous troll snarled, sitting in a seat several times too small for him. "What did we agree on?"

"No talk of the dragon," Sam'il said, and as suddenly as it stopped, the conversation resumed, loud and raucous as before. "Sorry, Red. We don't talk about that here."

"I didn't know you had such strong feelings about anything."

"Just one thing," Sam'il said slowly, holding up a gnarled finger. "One single thing that gets the craw of everybody in this place. They did not like being burned alive. Not one bit."

"Wait," Red leaned in and I followed. "These are the sam—"

Sam'il shook his head. "No, no, no. We don't talk about that here. We're just gonna serve beer and have a good time. Now, what can I get you?"

Red pulled two glowing, pink orbs out of a pouch in her belt. "Two large flagons."

The orc poured our drinks and handed them to us. Red walked us over to the far corner, where two gnomes skittered away from high back chairs near a roaring fireplace.

"This place is weird," I said, taking a sip of the flagon. The liquid was sticky like syrup. "What is this?"

Red took a sip of her drink. "It's whatever you want it to be."

"Oh," I replied, taking a sip of mine and finding it dull and tasteless. "It tastes like water to me."

"You're boring."

"Oh, if only that were true." I took another sip. This time it tasted like red wine, and with another sip it was cherry cola like my mother used to buy.

"You would want to be boring?"

"Are you kidding?" I said with a chuckle. "I would be home right now if I were boring. I would be doing school-work, in the back of our van, with a book, and maybe some hot chocolate, instead of here in Urgu with you. No offense."

"Only some taken," Red replied.

"Hey!" a man's voice shouted from across the room. "I recognize you. Both of you!"

"Stay calm," Red said, setting down her drink. "There is always one trying to make his bones, and I am a very popular target."

I knew the feeling of being a target. Back on Earth, monster hunters tried their hand at taking me down at least once a month, both for the prize they thought they would win, and the glory of killing the last gorgon. Whether that status was accurate was a matter of some speculation, but if there were other gorgons, they were hidden far underground; far enough that monster hunters couldn't till them up easily. I wasn't hard to find. Luckily, I was hard to kill.

"I have your back," I said.

Red stood, pulling two silver daggers out of her belt. "I have no quarrel with you, nor do I wish to have one."

The man lunged drunkenly against a chair and pushed himself up. It was then that I recognized the tattered cloak of the wicked witch's guard. I looked closer at his face. Though it was scarred on one side, his face was familiar to me. "I recognize you. You were a Captain. Captain…"

"Balsim!" the man said, his face gaunt and his beard thick. He swayed from side to side as he slurred his words. "I was the greatest captain in the Queen's Guard, and now, look at me. I am nothing. Cast away by the very army I was born to serve."

"It is not my fault you served the usurper," Red growled.

"Usurper!" Balsim slammed his foot down. "That little bitch in the castle stole her title from the greatest queen the Land of Oz has ever seen."

"Rose is the rightful ruler!" I shouted. "Hypnos blessed her!"

Balsim laughed. "She won't rule for long. In fact, with any luck…she's already dead!"

"What?" I shouted, stepping forward.

"Don't. He's trying to get your goat and rile you up," Red said, placing her hand on my shoulder.

I brushed her away and I kept moving forward, despite the crowd of men and monsters gathered around the Captain. "What do you mean, already dead?"

Balsim staggered toward me. "Do you know how many of us there are left, loyal to Queen Nimue? We gave up everything for her. We gave up our pride, our lives, and even our free will, on the promise of riches and salvation!"

"Then you should have hitched your wagon to a better horse!" I shouted back. "Now, what do you mean that Rose is dead?"

Balsim smiled. "We carried out an attempt on her life not twelve hours ago." He pointed to the locket around my necklace. "I recognize that magic. The queen has a similar mirror in her room. Look for yourself. It will confirm I'm telling the truth."

Balsim took one more step, but with nothing else to steady him, he fell onto the floor, unconscious. Meanwhile, I scrambled for the locket around my neck. I stared into the mirror and it spun for me in a million different colors.

"Show me Rose."

The mirror cleared and I stared into Rose's room; our room. Sitting on the bed was Rose, staring forward in shock and trembling. Her hair was matted to her face. Tears streamed down her face, leaving a trail in the ashes clinging to her. Her body was covered in soot.

"Something's wrong. I have to go back!" I said.

Red pulled me back. "You can't help her."

"Yes, I can!" I struggled to break free. "I'm the only one who can."

Red pulled me tighter. "The only thing that will help Rose is getting her out of Urgu forever, and you know it."

"You can handle this mission alone. I need to get to her," I said, snapping my arms and breaking her grip on me.

Red straightened herself up. "I appreciate your confidence, but even I will have trouble stealing from a god. Now, how badly do you want to go home?"

I looked up at her. "With everything in my being."

Red placed her hand on my shoulder. "Then you know what you have to do."

"If she dies, then I'm dusting you."

Red nodded. "You can try, but you will fail. Meanwhile, you are needed here, and you must hope that your bond with Queen Aine holds firm until we can get what we need and return. Agreed?"

I nodded. "Agreed, but no more of this messing around. We have to go, and we have to go now."

Red let me go. "Fair enough. Lead the way."

CHAPTER 12

ROSE

I sat in the silence of my room most of the night. At one point, I watched the mirror blink on, and for a moment I saw Chelle's face. I wanted so badly to scream for her, to beg her to come back, but I knew that if I asked, she would come. And if I asked her to come back, she would resent me the rest of our lives.

I would rather die than have her resent me…heh…it might come to that. Chelle always told me about the times that monster hunters came to take her life, and how she risked everything to fight them off. I had always hoped I would be so brave in the face of my own death, but all I could do was stare blankly and cry until there were no tears left to shed. I was not prepared to die. I did not want to die. I especially did not want to die in the Dream Realm, where my soul would disintegrate.

Maybe they were right, and I wasn't ready to be queen. Maybe it was time to go home.

There was a knock on the door, and it opened before I could open my mouth to speak. Queen Aine floated in, clad in a gold robe to match her golden headdress. I half wanted to thank her for saving me, and half wanted to interrogate her about whether she tried to kill me, but mostly, I found it impossible to open my mouth to do either.

"I know last night was troubling, my queen," Aine said. "But you must get up and face the day."

"Why?" My voice was shaky.

"Because if you hole up in this room for the rest of your life, then the plotters who work to take your life will win. They will know you are weak, and never stop coming for you. You must not let that happen. You must show that you are brave, and strong, which is why I called a meeting of your small council. They informed me that you haven't had one since you took over for Nimue. Nothing will show you are more in control than sitting across from the most boring people in the whole of Urgu and listening to them pontificate for hours on end."

"I'm sorry, small council?"

"Of course," Queen Aine said, floating toward me. When she finally caught a good look of me, her face contorted in disgust and disappointment. "Oh my god, have you been like that all night? You poor dear. I'll have the maids draw you a bath, and scrub you clean, and then we will pick out your most queenly gown and go down to the council chamber together."

"Council. Chamber."

Queen Aine took me by the hand and pulled me to my feet. "Of course, the problems of the day don't solve themselves. That is your job, to take care of the kingdom, and your small council will help you. What did you think the job of a queen was?"

"I don't know," I said, allowing Queen Aine to guide me toward the bathroom. "I have done nothing but greet well-wishers for weeks. I'm almost glad to know there is more to it than that."

"More, not much more, but more. Most of your job is to seem awake and alert while people ask you for things, which is a challenge in and of itself, and why I will make sure the valets bring you some Earl Grey tea to perk you right up."

"Thank you?" I said. I didn't understand why Queen Aine was being so nice to me.

"Tut tut. Think nothing of it. Once somebody took me under their wing and showed me how to be a queen, and now I get to carry on that great tradition."

True to her word, Queen Aine had two scullery maids draw me a bath. They scrubbed the ash out of my body and my hair. They brushed out my hair. They even painted my fingers and toes, and for an hour, I didn't think about Chelle. I didn't think about almost dying. I didn't think about anything except being pampered.

After I was done, Queen Aine had a surprise for me. She brought in a masseuse because she said I was too tense. I thought it was garish overkill, but if you couldn't have garish overkill as a queen, what was the point of the constant death threats and excessive tedium?

"What about the meeting?" I asked as I lay on the table, getting the best massage of my life, and suddenly, my desire to leave Urgu vanished into thin air. If this was the life of a queen, I could get used to it.

"Real power comes from being late and making powerful men wait for you. They will wait for as long as it takes for you to show up."

When the massage was finished, I slipped on a purple dress that Queen Aine laid out for me. One of my hand-maidens cinched up my corset and then tied me into the bustle. Finally, after three hours, I was ready for the small council, or at least as ready as I would ever be to confront a room of stuffy old nobles.

Queen Aine floated alongside me on our way to the meeting. Nimue had her part decorating this hallway, to be sure. Instead of the flowers that adorned the entranceway, these walls told tales of gargoyles and cemetery plots. The paintings showed visages of demons and monsters.

"Well, at least you look like a queen," Queen Aine said.

"That's something, right?"

"That is everything. If you can look the part, you can pretend to be the part. So, today, you just need to smile, nod, hear the council's concerns, and say 'no' politely. Can you do that?"

"Yes, just say no."

Queen Aine nodded. "And whatever you do, don't eat anything."

"Really?" My stomach growled. I knew I didn't have to eat, but my nerves said otherwise. "I'm so hungry."

"Too bad. We can eat later."

"What about drinks? I was promised tea, and I would really like some tea. Coffee would be even better."

"As long as you can drink without spilling, you may drink tea, but be demure about it." Queen Aine gave me a pointed look. "Can you be demure about it?"

I thought for a long moment. "...nebulous."

Queen Aine took a right before reaching the throne room through a small alcove I must have walked past a dozen times a day and never noticed. A short, plump guard stood at an ornate door, carved with busts of the Six. The Six were the gods imprisoned in Urgu—Hera, Sekhmet, Anansi, Agrona, and Loki—and Hypnos, the God of Dreams, who was their jailer. They had been trapped in

Urgu for thousands of years under his watchful eye. Of course, since he had vanished without a trace a hundred years ago, they had simply been trapped without a jailer, or anyone to tamp their baser instincts.

Queen Aine hovered in the guard's face, scowling at him, until he stepped aside and opened the door for us.

"That will never work!" A loud voice boomed through the chamber as we entered. Along the walls, there were carved busts of men and women whose faces I recognized from paintings throughout the castle, and there were tall pictures of regal-looking people slaying dragons and fighting bears.

A long wooden table stretched through the middle of the room. It was polished and shiny. Silver candelabras combined with the chandeliers above, and candles hanging from fixtures on the wall, to bring a surprising amount of light into the room.

"I'm sorry for our tardiness, gentlemen," Queen Aine said as she floated toward the head of the table, where a badger-faced man with buck teeth and a raggedy black toupee sat, his eyes bulging out of his head. His nose was four times as big as the rest of his body, and he reminded me of Pinocchio with his comically-oversized schnoz.

"I believe this is the queen's seat, Baron Cyrano," Queen Aine said with authority.

"Of course," the Baron replied. "We didn't think you would actually come. After all, every day for three weeks we have sent word, and every day for three weeks we have been rebuffed."

"Yes, well, that shall not happen again," Queen Aine said. "I am here now to advise the queen, and things will run considerably more smoothly from now on, I promise you that." She turned back to me. "Queen Rose, if you would join the others. I don't believe you've been properly introduced."

I stepped forward, careful that I did not step over my comically-oversized dress and trip. "No, I don't believe I have."

"This is Cyrano De Bergerac, master of foreign relations."

"How do you do?" Cyrano said, his buck teeth sticking over his lip.

"Charmed," I said.

"Yes, yes. Then moving around the table. This is Antonio, master of the purse." He was old, with eyes sunk into his head, wearing a long, black robe. His thin lips curled into a smile as he bowed. "Shakespeare once wrote a play about him and he hasn't shut up about it since."

"A pleasure to finally meet you, my queen."

"The same to you," I replied.

The final man in the room had a strong build. He towered over the others and didn't wait for introductions before stomping toward me. "Odysseus of Ithaca, my queen. A pleasure to make your acquaintance. You are more lovely and fair than even the greatest poets in Greece could do justice."

He kissed my hand, and I smiled at him, uncomfortably, before looking back at Queen Aine. She nodded. "Yes, Odysseus is quite the charmer. He's also the minister of war, which makes him the most useless member of your cabinet, as there hasn't been a war in some time."

I noticed a single empty chair next to Antonio. "Is someone missing?"

"The master of monsters was summarily dispatched by Queen Nimue," Antonio said. "My apologies, former queen

Nimue. Deposed queen Nimue, I suppose would be even more correct."

"Quite," I said, walking toward my seat at the head of the table. "And this is my small council. My entire small council?"

"That's right, ma'am," Cyrano said. "Until we can replace our master of monsters, of course."

I wanted so badly to point out that aside from myself and Queen Aine, there were no women on the small council. In fact, since Chelle and Red left, the only women I'd seen in the castle were maids and cooks. I kept my mouth shut as the Queen instructed me. There would be time for sweeping change after the coronation.

"Right," Queen Aine said. "Let's get to it. But first, can we please have some of that tea?" Queen Aine pointed to a tea pot in the middle of the table. "Yes, that one."

"Oh no, my queen," Antonio said, snapping his fingers. "That is far too cold for the likes of the queen. We will fetch another pot."

A young man entered the room, picked up the pot and the sandwiches around it, and then disappeared. Before a minute had passed a new pot appeared with a new batch of little sandwiches. I desperately wanted to eat the sandwiches, which looked delicious, but knew Queen Aine would scold me if I tried. I would make sure to order them to be brought back to my room for later.

"Let me, my queen," Cyrano said as he poured the tea for me.

"Thank you," I said, breathing deeply as the vapor hit my nose.

I lifted the cup to my lips, and out of the corner of my eye saw Queen Aine rushing towards me. She knocked the tea out of my hands.

"Hey!" I shouted. "What did you do that for?"

"I'm sorry, my queen, but I believe that tea was poisoned. Something was off in the way it smelled." She pointed to the place where the tea spilled, and we watched the liquid eat through the floor.

"Oh, come on!" I threw my hands in the air. "Can't I catch one break this week?"

CHAPTER 13
NIMUE

I followed the band of brightly-colored, nomadic Mountain People through the forest for the whole night. When the sun rose, they came to stop in a clearing five miles from the Gates of Droangor. As they walked, I overheard some of their complaints.

They had come down from Agrona's Mountains. Something was happening there that forced them to leave, but they refused to talk about it in detail. I just heard the word "them" repeated in hushed whispers. Whoever "them" was had forced all their kind to flee to the sanctity of the Gates over the past ten years.

We had dealt with refugees in the Land of Oz for as long as I was queen, but the problem had grown worse in recent years when the Mountain people started coming through the gates. They refused to explain why, though they insisted that they sought protection in the safety of Oz. I found them innately dangerous, if they were accustomed to surviving in the mountains, and had no interest in letting them assimilate into Urgu. This brought us to a stalemate.

We erected camps for them just inside the gates until a better solution could be found. From the looks of it, a better solution still hadn't been found.

It was not very compassionate, but I was not a very compassionate person. Compassion and power rarely mixed. There was nothing to be gained by helping those from other kingdoms. There was barely anything to gain by helping my own subjects, except to prevent a full scale mutiny and riot, or to save my own skin, and similarly, we did only enough to prevent the refugees from an outright revolt, while keeping them weak enough that we could easily overtake them if the need arose. The Mountain people were not to be underestimated. They survived in the harshest climate in all Urgu, with monsters that would cause the blood of even the most hardened of the Queen's Guard to go cold.

Sometimes, we mined the refugees for soldiers when we needed to take down some warlord or another. We'd promise a path to citizenship and land, but they were put on the front lines and fed to the meat grinder of war. Those that survived were dealt with on an individual basis to ensure they would not bring trouble to the kingdom. We could not have trained soldiers going back to the camps and infecting the others with their newfound skills. Only the absolute best, and those who gave their free will to me, were allowed to remain. So few chose to do so that it was almost not worth mentioning.

When the caravan stopped in the light of day, I squatted low in the brush. My legs were covered in scratches and my feet were bruised from walking through the woods. I was sticky from sap and dried blood.

"Set up here!" a woman called out. She had purple

threads of light running through her dreadlocks and her eyes shone red as she marched through the group of fifty or so men, women, and children. "We camp for the day and make the rest of the way by nightfall."

I sat down and watched them make camp. It wasn't long before the sweet smell of stew filled the air, and I was so hungry my roaring stomach might give away my position. I needed them to sleep so that I could steal some clothes, and possibly one of their masks as well. I needed to look as unlike myself as possible to make my way through the wall.

There was a chance that the men at the gates would be soldiers still loyal to me, but it was equally possible that Rose and her ilk had found a way to reverse my loyalty spell, the one binding their will to mine. If they weren't my soldiers, then I would be arrested immediately. Even if they were loyal to me, I certainly did not want to be seen naked as a jaybird.

It took an hour for the group to settle, tents and clotheslines marking the landscape. Everybody had a job, and each job was executed efficiently. It like a well-oiled army unit. There were no lost soldiers, or lost efficiency, even down to the smallest children. Some gathered firewood. Others hung clothes, while still others disappeared into the woods looking for water.

My eyelids were growing heavy when the group finally settled around the campfire for dinner. There was laughter and music, and I knew this was my chance. It would have been better to wait for them to sleep, but I needed to get clothes to get away from the group as soon as possible. Their joviality sickened me.

I crept forward into the camp. A sentry patrol turned

toward me, and I ducked behind a tent across from her to avoid being detected. Poking my head out to make sure the guard had gone, I hopped across to another tent. Behind the third tent was a clothesline. Much of the clothing hadn't been washed yet, and they sat in a pile next to a wash basin. I checked around the corner once more to make sure I was alone, and then dipped down to rummage through it.

It smelled something, as if they had been walking for a year straight without a break. Even the dry clothes were damp, but I found a dress that wrapped around my body well enough, and a pair of shoes that would suffice, even if their soles were worn through and their toes burst open. I ripped the cloth from the bottom of my dress and stuffed it into the shoes to make them fit better, but they still wiggled from side to side.

I might have looked foolish but at least I was clothed. Rummaging some more through the pile of laundry, I found a sash to tie off my dress so that I didn't have to hold it closed.

"What are you going?" I heard from behind me and leapt out of my skin. I turned to see a little boy gnawing on the leg bone of a squirrel.

I was no longer a queen and I had no powers. I had to play nice. "Me? Oh, I was just admiring your clothes."

"You have been following us," he said.

"Me? No. I haven't."

He nodded. "We're very good at tracking threats. You aren't one. I was told to offer to help if you came into our camp. We're refugees, just like you."

I looked around. "This is a joke, right?"

He shook his head. "No joke. Follow me, if you want."

It had to be a joke, or a trick, but I was too tired to fight him. If I still had my powers, I could easily take on fifty people, especially ones as gaunt as this lot looked, but as it was, I was barely able to stand. If I ran, I would have no chance of surviving in the woods by myself.

I had no choice but to follow the boy into camp. He had jet black hair tinged with a bright green, and when he looked back at me his flame green eyes were like those from a poison dragon.

"Do you like squirrel?" he asked.

I shrugged. "Dunno. Never had it."

"I hope you do."

When I entered the circle where the refugees ate, a hundred eyes turned to me. I had never seen anything like theirs before. They weren't hazel or blue or green like those I remembered from The Emerald City. They were on fire with bright hues that matched their hair, beautiful as they were haunting. The woman who was clearly in charge stood and walked toward me.

"Friend or foe?" she said, eyeing me up and down. It felt like her bright red pupils bore into my very soul.

"Would you believe me if I said friend?" I asked.

"That depends. Are you a friend?"

I paused for a moment. She was testing me. "I don't know. I am not a foe, but I'm not sure if I am a friend, either."

She nodded. "Fair enough. I appreciate your honesty and integrity."

Two things I have never been accused of before, being honest or having integrity. "Thank you. And who might you be?"

"We'll get there, but first, you look tired and weary," The more she spoke, the thicker her accent became. She was clearly Irish, and deeply Irish at that, with a thick brogue that gobbled up every word.

"I am."

"Then sit and eat with us."

This was another test, this time of just how desperate I was for help. "I'm sorry. While I appreciate the gesture, I do not eat with people I do not know."

She cocked her head, confused. "You would deny our friendly offer?"

"We do not need to eat, or sleep, even though our bodies tell us otherwise. I would love to eat...with a friend, but as a friend, you will tell me your name."

The woman smiled, silent for several seconds. "Very well. You may call me Boudica, Queen of the Mountain Tribe."

"Does that mean you were blessed by Agrona, since you are a queen?"

"She has never blessed any to carry on her work. She works in secret on the highest peaks. I won my queenship through hard fighting and hard drinking." The others chuckled at her words. "And who are you, then?"

I smiled. "You may call me Alice. I have been lost in these woods for many days, and I welcome the comfort of a friend."

I wasn't sure if she believed me, but if I revealed the truth of who I was, then she would surely not count me as a friend. After a quick nod, she walked back to her seat. "Very well, Alice of the Dark Domain. Sit, eat. You are safe here, or as safe as any can be in a place such as this."

I took my seat inside the circle. "Thank you for your kindness."

And I meant it, too. It might have been the first real thing I said in years. People acquiesced to me often, but they were not kind to me. They did what I said because of what I could do to them if they didn't, not because they wanted to. As the young boy with fire-green eyes passed me a bowl of stew, I reveled in the first nice thing that somebody had done for me in over a century, and I think I liked it.

CHAPTER 14
ROSE

I paced back and forth across the throne room for an hour
after my second attempted regicide in as many days. I
wasn't angry, even. I thought I would be angry, but I was
more confused than anything. Confused and hurt.

"Who could want me dead?"

Queen Aine was watching me with the kind of boredom
usually reserved for watching paint dry. "If you keep whin-
ing? Then me, for one."

I spun around toward her. "I'm serious."

Queen Aine shook her head. "You aren't going to want
to hear it, love."

"Yes, I do." I stomped my foot hard enough that it hurt
my heel. "How are we going to find the killer if you can't be
honest with me?"

Queen Aine floated toward me. "Oh, I can be honest. It's
just, that this display is quite unqueenly, and you are
acting, like…"

There was a long pause. "Like what?"

Queen Aine stared daggers at me. "Like a child."

I threw my hands in the air. "That's because I AM a child!"

Queen Aine scoffed loudly and rolled her eyes. "You're nearly twenty!"

"You just don't understand Earth," I said in a snit.

Queen Aine placed her hands on her hips and cleared her throat. "In my day, you would have three children and probably died in childbirth by now."

"Grim."

"Yes, it was. My point being that you are anything but a child. Even if I were to believe you a child on Earth, here in Urgu, you are a queen, and part of the problem is that you refuse to act like it."

"I'm trying," I said, throwing up my hands in the air again. "But it's hard."

Queen Aine nodded in agreement. "Of course it's hard, love. That's why not just anybody can do it, but it is your duty, if you do not want to get killed."

I was quiet for a few moments before I finally managed to say what was on my heart. "And what if I just...don't want to be queen?"

Queen Aine snorted. "Excuse me?"

"What if I don't want it?" I whispered. "Can't I just give it back?"

"That's simply not possible. Queenhood is bestowed by divine right, and yours was given by Hypnos himself. The only way to remove it is through death, or by his decree."

"But he's gone," I replied.

Queen Aine shrugged. "Then, I'm afraid you're stuck with it."

"Poop," I said with a sigh. "Fine. But as queen, I demand you tell me who's trying to kill me."

"Well, I don't know that, dear. I just know who wants you dead, because that part is easy."

I furrowed my brow. "Why easy?"

Queen Aine paused, enjoying the dramatic effect. "Because it's everyone."

"Everyone wants me dead? That's not fair! I didn't do anything to them!"

"None of this is fair, dear, but it's none the less true. Over the hundred years of Nimue's reign, she executed or exiled every royal who was loyal to Ozma, replacing them with sycophants and hangers-on who would grovel at her boot. Vanity truly was her greatest weakness."

"You were one of those hangers-on."

"I certainly was not!" Queen Aine boomed loud enough that it echoed through the room. I took a step back. "I am a queen, who partnered with another queen to get something she wanted—namely, a return to Earth—and no more. I had no allegiance to the queen of Oz then any more than I do—"

She stopped herself mid-sentence, but it was abundantly clear what she was going to say, so I stomped toward her. "Finish your sentence."

Queen Aine shook her head, looking down. "I don't want to."

"You were going to say 'now,' weren't you?"

"...Maybe."

I waited a long time before I spoke. "Why are you still here, if you feel no allegiance to me?"

Queen Aine met my eyes with a steely resolve. "Aside from the pact I made with your paramour?"

I nodded. "Aside from that. What drew you here in the first place?"

Queen Aine puffed out her chest. "It is customary for

someone of my stature to show her respect for a new queen."

"And what made you help me?"

"I don't understand the question. Your girlfriend—"

"She told me your deal. You were supposed to make sure I didn't die, not turn me into a queen, or advise me on protocol. So, why do all of this extra stuff if you don't even want to be here?"

Queen Aine nodded. "Very well, though it is the way of the Unseelie, I will not lie to you. I stayed because you are pathetic."

"Excuse me? I went from nothing to queen. I'm an inspiration."

"Going from nothing to queen, that makes you an *embarrassment.* I wish to return to Earth, but for now The Land of Oz is my home, and if you are to lead it, I will make sure you are a queen to be respected, not one to be killed." The look in Queen Aine's eyes was fierce and pointed for a moment, and then it softened. "Besides, the truth is, that, despite my better nature, I like you. You are kind...and gullible. You remind me of a wounded fawn. Chelle was right. I can't help but want you to succeed."

"You don't think I will survive being queen?"

Queen Aine fluttered closer to my face. "I think you can, with my help."

I turned away from her. "If everything's against me, then what should I do?"

"A show of force. Take the small council and dust them in front of the whole town."

"That sounds excessive. What if they are innocent?"

Queen Aine chuckled. "They worked for Nimue. They are anything but innocent."

"Still, that seems excessive, especially if they didn't do anything to me."

"Sometimes, excessive force is the right call."

I nodded. "Noted, but it doesn't sit right with me."

"As queen, you will have to make a lot of tough calls. A little bloodshed now will make the others think twice about crossing you."

I bit my lip. "Maybe, but I still want to dig around and see if they are guilty before I condemn them to death."

Queen Aine shrugged. "Fine, you ask my opinion but don't take it."

"I'm sorry," I replied. "I've never ordered anybody killed before. It sends my stomach into knots. I can't do it."

Queen Aine cracked a half smile. "You're too human. This place hasn't destroyed that part of you yet. Very well, we shall search for your evidence, and when you find it, the guilty parties will be put to death on your order."

I shook my head. "My order? Can't somebody else do it?"

Queen Aine blinked. "It needs to come from you. They must know you are strong, or they will never respect you. Nimue did not have everybody's love, but they all feared her and respected that she would do anything to maintain power. These conspirators are no different. They smell blood and are circling because they believe you are weak. You must show you are not."

I sighed. "Sounds hard."

Queen Aine smiled back. "It will be."

"So, where do we start figuring out who's trying to kill me?"

Queen Aine chuckled. "We? No, my dear. I have about a hundred things to do. I have a coronation to plan. But you, if you insist on continuing with this folly, should start in the kitchen."

"Why the kitchen?" I asked.

"That's where the poison came from. If I were you, I would want to know how poison left the kitchen without the royal taster trying it."

"Royal taster?"

"Of course, my dear. Every queen requires somebody to taste their food. Otherwise, there would be an attempt on their life every day." She made a shooing motion. "Off you go."

"Won't you come with me?"

Queen Aine sighed. "You have the powers of a God. If you cannot handle a couple of chefs, then I weep for you. However, I will make sure Balor joins you, if he is able."

"Thank you."

"And Rose?" Queen Aine said.

"Yes?"

"Please don't die. It would be very unbecoming of you."

CHAPTER 15
CHELLE

"I don't trust the Unseelie," Red said. "I just want that noted."

We were nearing the Enchanted Woods to meet Muirgen, the new captain of Queen Aine's guards. The letter we had from Queen Aine would tell her to transport us to the Gate of Droangor. The Gates led into the Dark Domain, the realm of Hera, and the last known location of the Wicked Witch.

"Well, we can't just ride there ourselves. How far did you say it was?"

"Three days, give or take," Red replied.

"Right, and meanwhile Rose is alone, guarded by the Unseelie queen, while we're dicking around on the Queen's Road for three extra days."

"A queen you made a pact with to protect her, correct?"

"I did, and that same queen gave me this letter."

"But she did not agree to protect you."

"No," I replied. "But her price was a favor from me in the future and that lasts until I return to the castle, so she has every reason to keep me alive."

"Unless she doesn't care about the favor," Red muttered under her breath. We were nearing the forest that would soon swallow us. Seven bulbs of light shone at the mouth of the woods.

"Then, she would still care about ending her servitude as quickly as possible."

"Halt!" a shrill voice cut through the tree line. "What business have you in the Enchanted woods?"

"We're looking for Muirgen," I replied.

Red and I had dealt with Muirgen before, unfortunately. She was one of my least favorite Unseelie in a long list of Unseelie which I neither liked nor trusted.

"What business do you have with the Seelie Captain?" the shrill voice asked. A pink ball of light floated toward us. The Unseelie never revealed themselves until it was necessary, especially to non-fairyfolk.

"Cut the bull, Muirgen," Red said, trotting past the ball of pink light toward one glowing yellow behind it. "Just show yourself already."

The ball of yellow sighed, and revealed itself as a fairy, holding a gleaming yellow sword and dressed head to toe in yellow. Her skin was yellow, too, and even the glitter adorning her body had a yellow hue to it, like urine after a night of drinking too much and not hydrating properly.

"Oh, it's you," Muirgen sneered. "What do you want?"

"We have a letter from your queen." I dug Queen Aine's letter from my pocket and held it out toward Muirgen, who flew forward to retrieve it.

"You expect me to believe you?" Muirgen scoffed.

Red glared at her. "Just because you are a liar, Unseelie, does not mean we all are."

Muirgen scoffed a second time. "Please, human. Your kind are the biggest liars in Urgu. We train for decades in the art of deceit and still have trouble with it, but lying oozes off your tongue as second nature. It just happens that we are convenient scapegoats. We've always honored our deals, unlike your kind."

"Is that what you told your Seelie brethren before you butchered them?"

Muirgen didn't respond to her. Instead, she unfolded the letter and read it. "And you haven't read this?" Muirgen asked, raising her eyebrow.

"How could I?" I replied. "It's written in your tongue."

Muirgen furrowed her brow. "Very well, then. And you wish me to follow these instructions exactly as written?"

"Is that a problem?" Red asked.

Muirgen shook her head. "No, but I want to be very clear with my words. You are the queen's confidants, are you not?"

"We are," I replied.

"I do not wish to start an international incident by sending you into the belly of the Dark Domain without your consent."

"That is our wish," Red said confidently.

Muirgen stared at the paper for another moment, and then held it out. The paper lit aflame in her hand. I looked over at Red, who simply rolled her eyes at the overblown theatrics of Muirgen's actions.

"Very well then, we shall away." Muirgen turned to the other balls of light. "Lieutenant Percival, you are in charge until I return."

A blue ball of light floated toward Muirgen but did not reveal itself. "Yes, captain."

Muirgen gave a quick salute and then turned toward us. "Close your eyes. You will feel ill when you land. That is normal but try not to throw up."

"Why?" I asked.

"Because it's unseemly," Muirgen replied. "And I have a very strong gag reflex."

"Just get on with it already," Red said, closing her eyes.

I followed her lead. I felt a great pressure weighing down on me, like I was being crushed in a pressure cooker, then I felt light as a feather, and then I felt nothing at all.

I was...gone. It was only then I feared for my safety, wondering if I had made a mistake trusting the Unseelie, but it was too late to turn back now.

CHAPTER 16

RED

There was a crackle in my ear, then a flash of light, and I appeared in front of the Gates of Droangor. Painted red and standing three hundred feet high, the gates towered over everything around, including the Wall of Itherium, which jutted out from either side of the Gates in both directions.

Protected by a battalion of Queen's Guard, the wall stood two hundred feet high and was topped with jagged parapets that prevented any from climbing over; the razor-sharp spikes would slice a finger clean off. Its sheer rock offered no footholds, just intricate runes carved into the rock to ward off magical creatures.

Further in the wild, where the wall crossed through the Forgotten Forest, there were rundown places to climb, but only from the inside. When you made your way back, you still had to scale the wall or beg for entrance, and that was if you could keep your sanity long enough to reach the far end of the woods. It was where I had climbed over in my younger days, though even at its most forgiving, the climb nearly killed me, and I only hung onto my sanity by a thread.

"Let's go," I shouted, turning to Chelle. She wasn't there. "Chelle!"

I spun around on my horse, but there was no sign of my Gorgon companion. I was alone.

"I knew it!" I spat. "I knew we should not have trusted that Unseelie trash."

I had to hope that Muirgen, trickster as she was, had delivered Chelle to Hera. There would surely be a price on her head. If I infiltrated the castle, I could save the Gorgon and arrest the Wicked Witch at the same time.

I trotted toward the Gates. Dozens of soldiers wearing the peacock of Nimue milled around, polishing their weapons and patrolling the grounds. In the distance, a collection of tents speckled the landscape. I couldn't make out the figures of those resting inside, except for a flash of blue, or yellow, or green, from their hair as they moved through the camps.

The Mountain People.

The neon in their hair was unique to their kind. Had I been closer, I would have surely seen the neon in their eyes as well. They were ferocious warriors and trackers, the greatest in all of Urgu, and I spent a year learning under them and their warrior queen, Boudica, in my time beyond the wall. *Why were they in Oz?*

The Gates of Droangor loomed larger as I approached. Inlaid in the gates were the faces of the Six; the cold stare of Hypnos, the penetrating sneer of Hera, the wry smile of Loki, the fiery madness of Anansi, the war cry of Agrona, and the roar of Sekhmet, each thirty-foot eye staring out into the distance, their watchful protection looking over the Land of Oz.

My heart leapt into my throat as I passed through the sea of soldiers. I knew they were in the service of Queen

Rose now, but these men had given their free will to Nimue. Who knew if word of her fall from power had reached this far from the Emerald City?

"What, ho!" I shouted, raising my arm to the large, dark-skinned soldier standing at the entrance of the Gates. On either side of him, large wooden towers reached into the sky. Atop these, four men worked the wheel to open and close the door to the outside. Even with four of the strongest men in Oz, it would take an hour to open the Gates.

"State your business." The soldier's moustache twitched as he spoke, and his words fired from his mouth with startling animosity.

"I wish to leave Oz and head into the Dark Domain."

"And you expect us to open the door to any that seek passage?" the soldier asked, crossing his thick arms across his chest. "Where is your order from the Queen?"

"Of which queen do you speak?"

"It doesn't matter if it's the old queen or the new, but unless you have passage orders from somebody in power, you'll have to wait until the next shipment from the Sandlands comes through, which should be in the next week or so."

"A week!" I crowed. "I cannot wait a week. Please, there must be something you can do."

The soldier shook his head. "These gates don't open without orders, or the promise of supplies. If you got neither, then there's nothing I can do."

"I don't believe you."

"That's smart of you," he said with a smile. "You're right, I could get them to open the door, but I won't."

"I come on business of the Queen. I must find Hera and the Wicked Witch at once. It is of the gravest importance."

The soldier rolled his eyes. "I'm sure it is, and that's why you'll have the papers we need to get the process started. Otherwise, you're just saying words, and words don't mean much at the Gates."

I didn't have any papers. I held my head up as high as possible. "Sir, I assure you that my word is my bond."

"I'm sure it is, but without papers, you're not getting through that wall, unless you want to climb, of course. We scraped a half dozen piles of dust off the walls this week. Men who thought they could climb. Not very forgiving, that wall. Course it was designed to keep people out...and in."

There was no use arguing with him anymore. I needed to find another way over the wall, even if it meant leaving my steed behind and taking my chances with the climb.

"Is there any rope?" I asked the guard.

"Not from us, I'm afraid. Maybe the refugees have some, not that it will help much. Those spikes at the top will cut your rope before you even start."

"I appreciate your concern," I said.

"It's not a concern for you. It's a concern for my men. It would be a shame if one as pretty as you got dusted."

"I assure you, I have no plans to die."

The soldier shook his head. "They never do."

CHAPTER 17

CHELLE

A flash of yellow light brought me back into the world from wherever we had vanished in the Enchanted Woods. The pressure on my body was gone, but so was my horse. I fell onto the floor and bounced hard on the stone underneath me.

Stone. Wait, that wasn't right. We were supposed to be at the Gates of Droangor. And it was dark. When we vanished, it was as bright as day. A yellow ball of light approached me. Muirgen.

"Where are we?" I asked.

"I'm sorry," Muirgen said, dropping her eyes.

I pushed myself up to my knees. "What are you sorry about?"

"You couldn't read the note, so you didn't know what it said."

"I know the deal Queen Aine made with me."

"Yes," Muirgen said, careful to stay out of the reach of my arms. "She was very clear, and, in fact, that is why you have been taken here."

I rose to my feet. "Where is here?"

"My castle." I heard, behind me. The voice was thick with power and yet smooth as velvet. When I turned toward it two purple eyes looked at me from the darkness. I had seen those eyes once before in the Emerald City and knew immediately that it was Hera who spoke to me.

"Your majesty," Muirgen said, bowing.

"You little rat!" I shouted, lashing out to strike, but then my arms wouldn't move, as if they were suspended by hands I couldn't see, held back by an invisible force that could have only been Hera's magic.

"Now, now," Hera said. "I abhor violence." She turned her attention to Muirgen. "What have you brought me, little one?"

"This is a gift for you, your majesty, on the condition that you leave Rose and the Land of Oz alone until after the coronation."

Hera paused. She looked like she was doing some calculations. "Interesting. And what is to prevent me from killing you and then killing her?"

"Oh, I don't think you want to do that," Muirgen said as sternly as her high voice would allow. "After all, this is the only body in all of Oz, and I am under strict instructions to murder her if you do not agree to my terms."

Muirgen wasn't wrong. I had what everyone else in Urgu wanted—a body.

"Wait...murder?" I said.

"Like I said, I'm sorry, but not too sorry," Muirgen said. "Just a little sorry."

"Why would you bring this...body to me?" Hera demanded.

"Once the fairies made a deal with your ward, Nimue, to exit the Dream Realm, but Nimue was weak and impetuous. She cared more about power and prestige, which is what made her an effective queen. It's also what made her a horrible subject."

"Yes, I did hate her so, especially toward the end."

"Can we bring this around to me?" I shouted. "I don't much like being bargained like a poker chip."

"Oh, Queen Aine doesn't play poker," Muirgen replied. "She prefers chess."

"Quite," Hera replied.

"Nimue believed this creature was the key to unlocking the Obsidian Spindle. Her girlfriend is to be crowned the Queen of Oz, and right now Queen Aine works to gain her confidence. With Chelle out of the way until the ceremony, and with your unsurpassed wisdom, you can find a way to use her unique situation to open the Obsidian Spindle. Then, between this Gorgon and the Dreamer, we can finally unlock a way home."

"Hrm," Hera said softly. "And you believe I can unlock in days what Nimue couldn't in a century. Why?"

"Because Nimue was only human, and her sensibilities and ambition only brought her so far. You are the greatest being in all Urgu, as powerful as Hypnos and as beautiful as Nox. Don't you agree?"

"No, I certainly don't!"

"She will need a muzzle," Muirgen said, glaring at me.

A mouth grew in the shadows, full of razor-sharp teeth, grinning broadly. "Very well, fairy, but you will stay with us as well, as my guest."

My arms fell to the ground, released by the invisible hands. "I'm not staying anywhere with you."

"Oh, I don't know about that. I see you hold the key to my library in your pocket. I'm sure you would like to see it, would you not?"

"Umm..."

"And if you should find a way to open the Obsidian Spindle and go back to Earth, why would you care if I were to join you?" Hera asked, more politely than she had ever said anything to me in our brief history.

"You want to destroy the Earth."

Hera's mouth turned down into a scowl. "Not the Earth. I don't care at all about your petty little planet. It is beneath me. I want the gods who locked me away. They don't care about you anyway."

"How can I trust you?" I asked.

"You trusted the fairies, and look where it got you? Here with me. I have no interest in lying to you. You are beneath me as an ant to an elephant. I offer you the knowledge you seek...for a price."

"And if I say no?"

"Your girlfriend is the most recognizable person in all of Oz. Until now, I've let her be, mostly because doing so amuses me, but also because I was plotting my next move. There is always a next move, and if I need to destroy your girlfriend to twist your arm, so be it."

"So, you're threatening me?"

"Not threatening, just stating a fact. I don't need either of you. You only survive for my entertainment, and to further this game."

"And if I stay, will you let me into your library?" I asked.

"You can go anywhere you like in this castle."

"Does that include where you are keeping Nimue?"

Hera chuckled. "I discarded that old hag weeks ago. She has failed me enough for a lifetime."

"You killed her?"

"Please, that would be too good for her. No, I took her powers away and forced her to suffer like a commoner. For one such as her, to whom power is everything, it was a fate worse than death."

I did not want to bargain with Hera, but it was either get dusted in the next five seconds or work with Hera and live to fight another day. I had to believe I could find a way out of this, if I just kicked the can down the highway for a little while.

"Very well, Hera. I accept."

"Of course you do, darling. It's not like I gave you a choice in the matter. Now come, we have much to discuss."

CHAPTER 18

RED

I ran my fingers along the grooved runes embedded into the Wall of Itherium. The runes were set there by Hypnos himself in a language that no mortal could understand, as much to keep warring factions and monsters out of Oz as to keep his citizens safe inside its borders. In the time before the wall, Ozians could set out to make their fortunes in the other realms of the gods, where they were often dusted, or turned against Hypnos under the charm of another god.

Urgu was supposed to be free of pain and pestilence. Hypnos wanted to create a utopia, where nobody wanted for anything, but once the old gods imprisoned their most troublesome kin inside of it, war was inevitable. The gods vied for power, worship, and a way to escape their confinement, and so Hypnos's mission became making his land, Oz, as safe as possible for inhabitants and travelers alike, while keeping the wars and petty squabbles of the gods beyond his walls.

Hypnos had one power above all others, and that was the ability to control Urgu. Even if he couldn't control where the dreamers came into the Dream Realm, he could create a beacon for them in the Emerald City of Oz and take control of the Obsidian Spindle. Dreamers rarely resisted the pull of the Obsidian Spindle, the only object in Urgu that could send them back to Earth or grant their deepest wish. Its pull attracted most all Dreamers to the Emerald City, and once they were there, he had to make sure they didn't make it back to the realms of the other gods.

If the gods were suffocated of Dreamers, then they could not build an army, and thus, they could not mount an attack on Oz. In that way, Hypnos could protect them, and by extension, himself, though he failed on that last point eventually.

The Land of Oz was the most populated of the six lands of Urgu, and the most metropolitan. The rest of the lands had loose associations of towns and federations, but nothing like the Emerald City. Small kingdoms sprouted up here or there under the supervision of the gods, where people banded together for the common good, at least until the nature of men tore them apart, or the monsters invaded. Mostly, the other lands were filled with nomads, and loosely constructed temporary cities.

I looked over at the encampments speckling the landscape. It was daylight, so the Mountain People were not out in droves. They preferred the comfort of night. Their hair was wild and laced with what they called neon, allowing it to glow in the continuous night of the mountain realm. Over the generations, their sorcerers connected with the dreams fueling all Urgu and witchcraft allowing the Mountain People to add the same neon to their eyes. Combined with their pale skin and the thick black clothing that covered them from head to toe, including their faces, they were a haunting sight.

They could be kind, too, as I had certainly learned in my

journeys, once I'd looked past their ghastly appearance. In the mountains, there were beasts and creatures most heinous, and it took a heart and body of stone to brave it, which meant that every inch of the mountain people was carved from marble. It took a lot to earn their good graces.

There were maybe two hundred of them in the camps, and I couldn't imagine there were too many of them left beyond the wall. There hadn't been another dreamer in a hundred years to replenish their ranks. Not that many people chose to join the Mountain People. The most hardened of the dreamers, back when they were still plentiful, sometimes longed for adventure and made their way to the Mountains and joined with Boudica's people.

The Mountain People's connection to the land is what kept them alive for so long; they had tapped into the magic of Urgu, within themselves. That was the scariest thing about them: They should not exist. They should not be able to harness neon, or make magic from nothing, or survive in the mountains, but they did all three, and thrived in even the harshest climates. This was certainly commendable, but it terrified me to my bones. I was the strongest person I knew in the Land of Oz, and I could barely hold a candle to a child of the mountains.

Perhaps they could help me find a way over the wall without heading into the Forgotten Forest, a day-long trek where I would battle the worst thoughts in my brain and hope to come out sane on the other side. If there was any rope to be had, or supplies, the Mountain People would have them.

Stepping foot in their camp, I made sure to be careful. One misstep could bring down their ire, and then there was no satisfying them without blood. A woman with blood red eyes tracked me across the camp. Her hair was so white it was nearly translucent. She sharpened an ax, and when she was satisfied it was sharp enough to gut me chest to navel, she stuck it into a sheath on the ground and picked up another.

After a long moment, her eyes drifted back to her work. Now I was being watched by a man with a long gray beard tied off at the bottom. His bright green eyes studied me as he cobbled a pair of black shoes.

"Red?" I heard a voice whisper behind me.

I nearly screamed out in terror when I turned around. I wasn't certain what was staring at me. Instead of a face, there was a porcelain mask with black eye holes. The mask was not in one single piece, but filled-in like an incomplete puzzle, with glass covering the exposed area. A gold wire mesh held porcelain and glass together, and behind the mask, black dust swirled like eddies in a tornado. The rest of the body was covered in a black cloak, and I dared not guess what was under it.

"Please, don't be frightened," the figure said. The mouth on its mask did not move. "Years ago, we met, and we traveled the Sandlands together looking for Hypnos, sure that a rumor about his being locked in a magic lamp was true. I did not look like this then, but you called me—"

"Shaina," I whispered. "My gods. Is it truly you?"

The porcelain mask nodded slowly.

"What happened to you, my friend?" I studied her while keeping my distance.

"I was dusted, left for dead, until the Soothsayer saved my soul, or what remains of it."

I gasped. "Dusted? And yet, you survived. How?"

"Come with me," Shaina said. "And we can talk about it over tea."

She started to move away, but I stayed put. "I'm sorry, but I don't believe you are who you say you are."

"I understand that. If you hope to find your friend again before she falls into darkness, then I suggest that you follow me."

"I don't know—"

"Please, for the sake of your Gorgon friend, come with me."

My brow furrowed. "How do you know of Chelle?"

"We know a great many things more than that. Come with me now and speak with the soothsayer."

I didn't know if I could trust Shaina, or even if she was truly my friend, but I needed help. They could have been preying on that trust, but I made my life out of following my gut, and my gut said to follow, so I did.

"Very well," I replied. "Lead the way."

CHAPTER 19
NIMUE

I woke up after what felt like days, my head throbbing and my eyes bleary. I tried to move my arms, but they were stuck together unnaturally with a metal clasp. A sticky goo prevented me from moving my mouth

"Try not to move," a voice said above me.

There was a loud thud and I was sent hurtling into the air. I knocked my head on the ground when I landed. I groaned and tried to move my legs, but realized they were also bound by a metal clasp.

"Did you think we would not recognize you, Nimue?" the voice said. My eyes focused on Boudica, who was pulling my carriage with her own strength, grunting with every movement, but never slowing down. Above me, makeshift iron bars separated me from the world.

I was powerless, and thus, their prisoner for the duration until they saw fit to release me. This was what Hera wanted, of course, for me to pay for my misdeeds through both torture and humiliation. I wondered if she watched what was happening with a wicked smile on her face.

"You should not struggle," Boudica said. "We will be at

the gates soon enough, and with you as a bargaining chip, they will surely let us through."

I craned my neck to look out. The Walls of Itherium rose in front of me, and the Gates of Droangor were nearly on top of us. Behind me, I expected to see a string of Boudica's refugees, but there were only two burly guards on either side of me, in case I should somehow escape. They were foolish to think it would take more than one to restrain me in my present state. I had no way of defending myself. I slumped back to the floor.

"The others will be along soon enough," Boudica said. "Not that you care, but you will set in motion a chain of events allowing the rest of my people to enter the gates. I have spent the last decade guiding them to the camps beyond the wall. There are not many left. When I strike a deal with the queen's soldiers, and my men go back to fetch them, they will be safe."

She was right—I didn't care, but she kept talking anyway. Her voice was gravelly and piercing. I hated it, but with my mouth glued shut I had no way of telling her to be quiet.

"Did you know that our people have been living in filth and squalor inside the gates to The Land of Oz for the last ten years of your reign, and you did nothing to help them?"

I did know that, but again, I didn't care.

"Today, you will atone for your sins against my people."

CHAPTER 20
RED

Shaina pushed open the flap of a green tent and I ducked down to enter it. The outside of the tent was dusty and bland, but the inside looked like a gilded bazaar, complete with dozens of statues of the Six, and plush ornamental rugs lining the ground. In the middle of the tent, a shrouded figure stared into a glowing red fire.

"I have brought her, Mother," Shaina said as she approached.

My eyes widened. "Mother?" I said.

Shaina did not look back at me when she spoke but kept her eyes on the woman. "The soothsayer birthed me a second time, and so in that way, she is my mother. I would not exist without her."

The soothsayer spoke in low raspy voice. "Good, my daughter." The shroud tilted up, and two bright golden eyes peered out, studying me. "You are smaller than I thought."

"I'm average height," I replied, slightly offended. "At least for my time."

The light licked her face but didn't bely the shadows

which hid her. "The way people talk, you should be twenty feet high, with arms the size of mountains."

I chuckled. "I appreciate that tales of my lore reach beyond me."

"You should. My people do not speak of many outsiders with the respect they reserve for you." The woman extended her stiff arm. It was black as sackcloth. "Please, sit."

So as not to offend the soothsayer, I took a seat across from her. Shaina helped pull back the woman's hood. Just like Shaina, her face was a mixture of porcelain and glass, but her eyes still glowed golden behind her mask, while Shaina's remained black and blank.

The porcelain of the soothsayer's skin was more ornate than Shaina's, painted with bright flowers that contrasted her otherwise dark appearance. When she spoke, her lips didn't move, but the ash behind her mask pulsated with the sound of her words.

"Shaina tells me that you saved her," I said. "Is that true?"

"It depends on what you meant by saved," the soothsayer said. "I contained her essence in a vessel, but if the vessel is punctured, her soul will drift off into dust like any other."

"How did you do it?" I asked breathlessly. "How did you do that which is impossible?"

"Nothing is impossible. If dreams are real, then we can do anything. If this place exists, then, by definition, nothing can be impossible. All we have to do is tap into its essence."

I had long known about the Mountain People's connection to the magic that powered Urgu but had never imagined something like this. "So, you used the dreams themselves to craft Shaina's visage?"

"And the magic around us," the soothsayer added. "And the very air we breathe. All of it is magic. None of it should not be possible, and yet it is. It is a form of soul binding, but instead of binding a soul to a person, I bind it to an object."

"The end result is fascinating, unexpected, and should be wholly impossible. Once a soul is dusted, it should drift off into the ether."

"Nothing should do anything in this place. Our minds cannot comprehend what this place is capable of."

"If you can do this, you can do anything," I said.

"I wish it were so. I have failed to save more souls than I care to remember. Still, over the years, this process has kept some people alive, even if we struggle to survive. Or at least it kept them alive until the attacks."

"How do you survive, though, if you are made of porcelain and glass?"

"The same way porcelain and glass have always survived: carefully. That was why we trekked across the mountains to Oz, so that we could survive." The woman's voice was thick with sorrow. "We are the last remaining two. One day, we are destined to die, too, but then, that is not what you are here to learn, is it?"

"No, I suppose not." I frowned. "I have no idea what I expect to learn from you."

"You would like to know about your friend, and how to find her."

I nodded.

"I have followed the Gorgon closely ever since she entered Urgu. Like me, she is an affront to everything that should be possible in this place."

Shaina pulled a snake's fang from the soothsayer's robe and placed it next to the fire. "We have watched her as best we could, when possible. We saw the trickster Muirgen taking her to Hera's castle."

"Hera!" I spoke in a harsh whisper. "That fiend!"

The woman sighed. "Yes, even now Hera plans to turn the Gorgon onto her side, but Chelle is strong, and with luck she will survive."

"I must go to her!" I said, standing.

The woman raised her arm, slowly. "You could do so, but your part to play is not there. It's here."

"How can you say that?" I asked, my words tinged with venom.

"Because even now, one comes that you are looking for. She crests over the final ridge in the Dark Domain and makes her way to the gates. She, who was once with great power but now without, is making her journey home."

"You're talking about The Wicked Witch?"

"Yes. Even now, Nimue closes in on us, and soon she will pass through the gates. She is the secret to everything. She is the key to saving Rose, and Chelle, and bringing balance to this world."

"No, she's the one that threw us out of balance."

The soothsayer took a deep breath. "It is easy to blame that on her, but she was just using the power granted her in the vacuum of Hypnos's absence."

"Wait, are you saying she can help us find Hypnos?"

There was a long pause. "In her way. I'm afraid that is all I can tell you without tipping the scales and changing the future."

"But...even telling me that—"

"I do not make the rules of magic," the soothsayer said with what looked like a shrug. "I just follow them as carefully as I can, as my power is tenuous. If I reveal more, then there will be disastrous consequences. All I can tell you is you must go to the wall and wait for the exiled queen to arrive. When she does, don't let her out of your sight."

"Thank you," I replied, pushing myself up. "This has been most unhelpful, and yet somewhat helpful at the same time."

"As is the way of magic." The soothsayer turned her golden eyes back to the fire, and I lost sight of them under her shroud.

I wished, in that moment, that magic was straightforward. If it could lay out a linear, solid path, I would follow it, but more often than not magic was merely a feeling and a vague pull in one direction or the other, and you don't know what it was trying to say until it was too late.

"That's why I prefer a dagger to a spell," I said, turning on my heel to exit the tent.

With a dagger, you knew what it was capable of, and it worked the same every time. Still, I was grateful to magic that at least I received some information. Chelle was alive. I had to hope she could withstand the persuasion of Hera and make her way to freedom while I dealt with Nimue.

The Wicked Witch needed to pay for her crimes. Once she was bound and imprisoned, then I could go back for Chelle.

CHAPTER 21
CHELLE

"I thought you were going to kill me," I said to Hera. We walked down a hallway in her dark, dank castle. The place was sparsely lit, and I had a feeling that was exactly as intended, as Hera liked to move through the shadows.

My snakelike ancestry gave me a couple of gifts, including the ability to see well in the night, which kept me from knocking into the castle walls. The light from Muirgen's body gave me a sense of the hallway around me, but the light didn't extend to Hera herself, no matter how hard I tried to make her out in the shadows. I wasn't even sure she was walking. For all I knew she floated because all I saw were her eyes. Light, what little light there was, seemed to avoid contact with her.

"That would not be very hospitable," Hera replied.

"I never took you gods for a hospitable lot."

"Please," Hera scoffed. "We are as hospitable as humanity deserves, which is not very. Your squabbles are so pedestrian, and you lose the forest for the trees, as the saying goes. I have watched it on planets across the cosmos."

"Planets?" I said, surprised both at the revelation and the casual manner in which she said it. "So, there is life on other planets?"

Hera's purple eyes fell on me. "This surprises you?"

"I mean, yeah?" I asked, confused. "Why wouldn't it?"

"You are in the presence of a god, and this is what causes you excitement? See, that is why I give humanity such little respect."

"I'm sorry," I replied. "But I'm not human, you know? At least, not all human."

Hera arrested her movement and turned to me. "No, you aren't, are you? And yet, you are the most human thing that exists in this place. Imagine what you could do with the power of a god."

I stopped in the hallway with her. "Is that what this is about? Giving me your blessing? Because I have no interest in joining you. I would rather die."

A slight smile appeared under Hera's luminous eyes. "That can be arranged."

"I won't wait around to die. *Fulminis!*" I shouted. A flash of lightning darted across the hallway, sending an electric blue glow through the dark, but passed right underneath Hera's eyes. "*Sonum augue!*" I pushed my hands together as a fireball grew in my hands and I threw it down the hallway. When it reached Hera, the darkness pulled it into two pieces.

"This is cute," Hera said. I heard her yawn. "And I do appreciate the display, but do you really think your third-rate magic could defeat a god?"

"I defeated Nimue with it."

"As I recall, she had you pinned against a wall, begging for your life, before your paramour saved you."

I dropped my eyes. "That's a fair hit."

"You could not defeat her when she wielded only a fraction of my power. Please believe you are only alive at my pleasure."

"Then why not kill me?" I replied.

"Why not kill the fly that buzzes around your head? Because you have not irritated me enough yet to warrant my wrath. Now come, I have something to show you."

She continued down the hallway and, with a sigh, I followed. In the distance, two candles burned, and their mild light felt like the sun in the castle's dark walls.

"Where are we going?" I asked.

"This may surprise you, but our goals are aligned. I have no interest in hurting anybody in Urgu, except maybe Hypnos. My only goal is to get back to Earth."

"And destroy everything."

"Not everything, just my cheating husband and the harem of godly sycophants who imprisoned me here for no reason than that I refused to be under his thumb."

"Zeus is the bad guy?"

"Have you ever read history? Of course, he is. I am vengeful, but rightfully so. My ire smites those who have disrespected me by daring to be born by the hand of my vile husband."

"History? Don't you mean mythology?"

"All history is mythology to somebody, sweetheart." We reached the candles on the wall, and Hera's black cloak revealed itself to me bouncing against the light of the candles. She ducked underneath the doorway arch and ducked inside. "Come."

I felt not unlike I had when I read Poe's work in high school, as if the looming dread of my situation would soon destroy me and my hubris. Hera was cruel, but she was more powerful than me, and one of the most powerful beings in Urgu. I had to be careful not to irritate her.

The archway was small and narrow. I had to turn sideways to fit inside, but when I did the room expanded into the distance for as far as I could see. Each wall was lined with shelves filled with old, leather bound books. Stretching into the vast expanse before me were tables and more bookcases. I was agog at the sheer scope of the collection.

"This is the wisdom I have accumulated over the years. Every book and tome on this gods-forsaken rock about how to leave Urgu. Nimue spent many weeks lost in these stacks, trying to find the answers, and came up empty every time. Every clue a dead end; every tactic, folly."

I looked over at her. "If that's true, what do you want me to do?"

"You bring fresh eyes, and, perhaps, a beginner's luck."

"That's just superstition," I replied.

"No, it's not. I should know. I invented it. Now, get to work. With any luck, we can save your girlfriend and set me free. Unless, of course, you would rather be dusted."

I thought for a long while. *Was I ready to make a deal with Hera, help her escape, in order to save Rose?* I promised I would do anything for her, but this felt like a step too far. Still, the knowledge of the gods was at my fingertips, and I didn't have to steal it. It was freely offered.

"There is only one rule," Hera replied. "No book may leave my sanctuary for any reason. Is that understood?"

That was going to be a problem. The book I needed was one I couldn't read without Rose, and I would never bring her here. I could sell my own soul, but I wouldn't put her in danger, too.

"What happens if I take something?"

"Then, the shadow demons will hunt you down."

"Shadow demons?"

Hera snapped her fingers and hundreds of yellow eyes opened in every shadow in the library. "My pets. The only things in this place that have never disappointed me."

I nodded. "I guess I won't be taking anything, then."

"Good. See how pleasant this can be if we all just work together?"

Then, she closed her eyes, and she was gone. In the shadows, hundreds of yellow eyes disappeared along with her.

CHAPTER 22
ROSE

I liked kitchens.

They were warm, inviting, and smelled good. Somebody was always making something delicious to eat. I used to sit in the kitchen and watch my mother cook. It was the only time she was truly giving or kind. She would teach me how to make things, and ask my opinion, two things she never did anywhere else in the house, or in my life.

Often, I snuck into the campus dining halls and just watched the cooks make meals. I couldn't afford to eat most days, but nobody could stop me watching. In Urgu, there was little call for food, but the chefs cooked anyway. Nobody had to eat, which made eating a luxury, and that made it desirable. Even before I was queen, I knew that rich people liked doing things that were desirable, which meant there were dozens of cooks in the kitchen at all times, even though it wasn't prudent.

"Excuse me?" I said meekly, and nobody paid attention to me, even though I was the queen, and was entering their kitchen for the first time since the start of my reign. "EXCUSE ME!"

This caused the kitchen to stop for a moment, but then most of them again went about their work. A short man with a face like a child waddled up to me. "Yes? Why do you disturb the kitchen?"

"Disturb?" I replied. "I am the queen. I don't disturb anything, and if we are picking nits, then this is my kitchen, as all of Oz is mine to rule."

"Queen?" the child-man said with a stutter. "I'm—sorry. It has been such a short time and we were never introduced. I've been preparing night and day for the coronation. Please, don't cut off my head or turn me to dust."

I chuckled. "I have no intention of doing that."

"Did you come to look over the food for the coronation? I promise you it will be a menu to die for."

"Interesting choice of words, given why I am here."

"I don't understand."

"So, you don't know that there was an attempt on my life earlier dealing with a pot of tea that came from this kitchen. I was almost poisoned, meaning somebody wasn't doing their job."

A loud gasp came from the kitchen staff. They all looked at the child-chef, who stuttered some more. "N—no, we had no idea. Nobody told us of any problems. We are—oh my goodness, we are mortified."

"Few people knew. Then there have been no other complaints from the rest of the castle?"

The chef shook his head. "Not that I am aware of, and I believe that if somebody was murdered this day, I would have heard it. My chefs are notorious gossips and busybodies. You know, wine and food go together with gossip like, well, wine and food."

"Uh huh. Where is the royal taster? They are supposed to taste everything before it comes to me."

The chef shrugged. "She never showed up today. It's not uncommon for tasters to fall ill, or worse, on the job, so we thought nothing of it. It's a shame. Gwendolyn was my favorite. She had an exquisite palette, one wasted on such a banal job." After the words came from his mouth, he clamped his jaw shut. "Sorry, your majesty. It is a very important job, but she was always so kind with her words. She could pinpoint the slightest variety of spice I used. I hope nothing happened to her."

"Do you know where she lives?"

The chef nodded. "Of course. There is a suite for them above the kitchen. A taster's life is short, so we show them the courtesy of luxury while they are with us."

"How long does an average taster last?"

"A year, sometimes. With the last queen, a taster would be lucky to last a week. Between the backstabbing on the court and the queen's whims, it was common to see the girls go like the wind, not that anybody lasted long in those days."

"You did."

"That is because I am the best. I was blessed with perfect taste, satisfying to everyone. Not to mention, I keep my nose out of the comings and goings of the court. That is my true superpower. The others gossip, but I keep my head down and do my work well. That is how I survive."

I nodded. "Thank you. Can you please point the room out to me?"

"Surely," the chef replied. "In fact, I will do you one better and guide you there myself."

CHAPTER 23
NIMUE

There was no comfort in the back of the wagon. It banged around until we reached the Gates of Droangor. I was almost relieved when the cart stopped at the entrance, and Boudica released the handles, dropping me onto the ground.

I watched as Boudica spoke with the guards. It wasn't a minute before they were marching back over toward us.

"See," Boudica said, pointing to me. "Here she is, your exiled queen, and I bring her back for trial in exchange for the safety of my people. You told me you would not let more of my people through the gates, but I ask you to reconsider with this gift I bring."

They wouldn't allow more of Boudica's people through the gates? I never approved that dictum. I wanted the Mountain People to share with me their magic and their knowledge if I were to grant them the kindness of my protection. *Was this Rose's decree?* That would make me laugh.

"I mean, it kinda looks like her," one of the guards said,

scratching his metal helmet. "But you can dress a pig up like a princess, and—"

"How can you say that with such disdain?" Boudica growled. "She is a spitting image."

"Can she do any magic to prove it?" the other guard replied, biting his fat lip. "I mean, the queen has powers, right?"

"No, she can't." She pointed to my mouth, which was still bound in goo. "She's a bit tongue tied at the moment. Listen, I am sure that you are quite busy, and while I am certain this is Nimue, if you need more proof, let me bring her inside the walls and you can conduct your own investigation."

"That does sound fair," the first guard said. I couldn't believe how dumb they were, that they would not recognize their own queen. *How could I have hired such incompetence?* They were a disgrace to the green peacock on their uniforms.

"I only ask that you allow me and my men to pass through, and if she proves to be the Wicked Witch, which I assure you she will, that you grant the rest of my tribe, the last of the Mountain people, to seek protection inside the land of Oz."

"Oof," the fat lipped man said, furrowing his brow. "I don't think I can make that promise. It's a little over my pay grade, but I think I can let you in, and then you can take it up with the watch commander."

"Very well," Boudica said. "Lead the way."

Boudica lifted my wagon again and followed the soldiers to the wall. It took twenty minutes to open an entrance through the gates big enough for the soldier to squeeze through, and another ten before they came back out and waved us inside.

A short guard ran up to Boudica. "I talked to my captain and he's gonna set you up with a nice cell for the prisoner, and then conduct talks with you."

"Wonderful," Boudica said, turning to me. "It looks like you might be completely worthless after all."

Worthless? I had kept the Land of Oz together for over a hundred years. No worthless person could do that, no matter what Boudica and her ilk cared to believe.

As I passed under the Gates, the faces of the gods mocked my plight. I turned away from them, and caught the face of an old acquaintance, the Red Rider, scourge of my time as queen, scowling at me, ready to thrust her daggers into my throat.

This day just kept on getting more and more interesting. I wondered vaguely what would happen to me next. Hera was probably getting a nice laugh at the way I was being treated. I, meanwhile, was less than amused.

CHAPTER 24
CHELLE

"How can you find anything in here?" I muttered to myself, holding the key that Queen Aine had given me. "There are a billion books, but zero doors."

"Perhaps I can help." I heard from behind me. I turned to see Muirgen floating just out of arm's reach. She must have known I would kill her if she came any closer.

"You want to help me, after you brought me here for Hera?" I said, lunging toward her. "I should kill you now."

"You wouldn't dare," Muirgen growled. "If you did, you'd never get out of here alive."

"Out of here?" I said, surprised.

Muirgen tentatively floated closer to me. She clapped her hands together, and a bubble grew from her hands and enveloped us. "We shouldn't say anything, not with so many eyes watching us, but yes. This was the queen's plan all along."

"Oh, I know," I said. "She's a devious bitch who I'm going to kill after I rip you apart."

"Did you really think you could sneak your way into Hera's castle, child?" Muirgen scoffed. "Did you think she wouldn't have a thousand safeguards in place? The only way for us to get you in was to make it look like a gift, a sacrifice, from Queen Aine to Hera."

I arched my eyebrow. "So, she's not tricking me?"

"She probably is, but not this way. She's trying to help you find the book, so we can open the Obsidian Spindle, and all go home. Wasn't that the plan?"

"It was," I replied, dumbfounded.

"Then follow me."

Muirgen's light glowed brighter as she led us down the aisles of books. She led me through all sorts of corridors then stopped in front of a door.

"Give me the key," Muirgen said.

"Yeah, right."

"I know you don't trust the fae, but you cannot open that door."

"Why not?"

"I can feel the power coming off of it. Nimue protected it with every ounce of her power so that only she would be allowed inside." Muirgen pointed to the grooves on the door. "These are runes written in fae, warning all to stay out. I cannot break them for you. It is a magical power beyond even my control. Only the fae stand a chance of not being completely evaporated by this magic."

I growled, realizing I would have to give up the key. I held on to it for a moment as Muirgen tried to pry it from my unwilling fingers, and then let it go, sending her flying backward into a stack of books.

"Mature," Muirgen grumbled.

She popped the bubble that contained our words and fluttered to the door. As she placed the key into the lock, her body began to convulse. She stifled a scream.

"Are you okay?"

"N-n-n-n-o!" Muirgen shouted. The lock flipped, and the door swung open. As it did, a hundred yellow eyes looked at us in the darkness and swarmed forward. "Hurry."

"*Lux*," I whispered, and light from my hand filled the room. There was only one book there, a shiny, golden one. I flipped it open. Its pages were blank, just like Queen Aine had said they would be.

"Chelle." Muirgen's voice was weak. She was breaking apart into dust. "Now."

I lifted the book. Given its size I expected it to be heavy, but it was light as a feather, though large and awkward in my hands. I made my way to Muirgen.

"I can't bring you back all the way to the castle. My magic is barely holding me together. You'll get to the woods, and then you'll be on your own."

"But—"

I didn't have time to say another word before we vanished with a crack of light. When my eyes regained focus, I was in the dark woods below Hera's castle. There was no sign of Muirgen, except for a cloud of dust.

There was no time for mourning, and I wasn't sure I would mourn if there was time, either. Muirgen was a jerk, even if she did help me in her last act. Lightning cracked and Hera's castle lit above me for a moment, ominously. I needed to reach the Gates of Droangor before Hera and the shadow demons found me.

I doubted the goddess would take it upon herself to track me down; not with so many lackeys. She did not seem like the type to handle these things herself. I had escaped, but I needed to be on the lookout for any sort of beastie that went bump in the night.

I pulled the book close and pounded my legs away from the castle, my stomach lodged in my throat with a combination of fear and adrenaline.

CHAPTER 25
RED

"I demand to see Nimue," I said, stomping into the office of the Watch Commander, who sat with the red-eyed queen of the Mountain People, Boudica, whom I broke bread with on my trips to the Mountains, and who helped me learn to track and stay alive in the wilderness.

"And I don't care, Belle," the commander replied. "I don't care that you're the queen's lackey any more than I care that the woman sitting in front of me is a queen."

Boudica and I both shouted in unison. "Hey!"

The watch commander looked over his wire-framed glasses at me. "It is my duty to bring Nimue to the castle for interrogation and questioning. I won't have you hurting her before then."

"I'm not going to hurt her. I just want to question her."

"And then hurt her," Boudica added with a twinkle in her neon eyes.

"Only if she breathes," I said with my own wry smile.

"Great," Boudica said. "Even more reason to give in to our demands. Because unless you agree that Nimue is still my prisoner, I could let Belle at her. Or I could slit her throat and dust her right now, which might be more merciful."

"Don't you dare," I replied.

"Relax," Boudica said. "It was a joke. Mostly."

"Oh. I didn't know you joked."

"Don't worry. I'm very aware you don't have a sense of humor."

"Ladies!" the watch commander shouted, slamming his hairy fists on the desk. "Do I have to separate you?"

"Likely." I appreciated Boudica's fierce resolve, even if she was rough around the edges. She had the temerity to exist in the harsh wasteland of the Mountains and look out for her people. She did not have to help me when I escaped the Land of Oz, and yet she took pity on me.

"I'm not asking for much," Boudica said, turning to the watch commander. "Just a safe place for my people in return for the delivery of a dangerous criminal to the realm."

"And we appreciate your service," the commander replied. "But I can't just let a hundred more of you refugees through the gate. We're at capacity."

"Please! What is capacity?" Boudica said, throwing her hands up. "There's nothing but space in Oz, and we're dying out there. The lands beyond your borders are getting harsher, and soon enough they will gobble us all up."

"Exactly why we can't just give asylum to every refugee at our gate. If we give it to you, then we have to give it to those from the Sandlands, and the Mistreach, and the Bogs too. Where will it end?"

"I don't care where it ends for them," Boudica snarled. "I care where it ends for my people."

"What exactly...is this one telling you?" I asked, realizing I had stepped into the middle of a conversation I knew nothing about.

"I offered the Wicked Witch in exchange for my people's safe passage through the Gates of Draongor, and for the release of those already here from the protection of the royal guards."

"And he refused?"

"Aye, he did," Boudica said.

"I'll make that deal," I replied.

"On whose authority?" the watch commander roared.

"By order of Queen Rose," I said with all the authority I could muster. "I am her emissary, and thus, I speak for her. Nimue is the most dangerous criminal in the realm, and while she might not matter to those who served her in the past—"

"Excuse me!" the watch commander pressed his hands firmly on the table.

"You heard me," I said, raising my voice. "You served the dark queen. You wear her colors, and her emblem. You are no friend to the Land of Oz, but this woman has brought us the worst criminal in the realm. We will honor her request. If you demand a written letter from the queen herself, I can arrange that."

The watch captain looked at me with white-hot anger. If he could use magic, fire would have blown out of his nose. "Very well. I suppose I have been overruled."

"Yes," I replied. "You have." I turned to Boudica. "Lock her in the jail cells behind this building. I will keep her here until your people are safe within the walls, and then I will bring her to the queen for trial. Is that fair?"

Boudica nodded. "Very fair, and thank you."

"It is my pleasure. Nothing will make me happier than

watching the false queen dusted in the middle of the Emerald City for all to see."

"Aye, she has been the scourge of my people, too, so I look forward to the day where we are rid of her for good, but until then, it is enough to know she will suffer great humiliation for her betrayal of Urgu."

We shook hands, and Boudica pulled me close for a hug so powerful I thought I might die. It was the first time I had been shown affection by the Mountain people, or honestly, by anyone, in a long time, and it felt nice. Even when I left the Mountains for what I thought was the last time, Boudica did not so much as nod in my direction.

Boudica gave a deep sigh and blinked back a tear. I could tell it had been a long time since somebody outside of her tribe showed her a human kindness. The Mountain people showed no emotion, so her briefly breaking down her defenses was unprecedented.

I smiled, inwardly. Most people did not feel safe to let their guard down around me. It was nice that one person did.

CHAPTER 26
NIMUE

Ow. Every inch of my body hurt. I felt like one big bruise after they pulled me out of the wagon. The camp was dirtier and dingier than I imagined it would be, but it bustled with the sounds of men hard at work.

My men. Once they were my men. Now, they were dragging me off to a prison cell. They had pledged their loyalty to me; their will to me. Now, they worked for Rose, even though they still wore the emblems that I designed.

I wondered if the men in the castle still wore the white peacock of Hera on their garments. She couldn't turn a corner without being reminded of my reign. The thought of it brought a smile to my face.

A guard with brown eyes and a scowl opened the door and, as his lanky partner waited outside, he pushed me into the jail and followed behind me. The jail was small, with little more than a drafting desk, a small rug woven with an image of Hera and Agrona in gold relief, and a jail cell that took up much of the room. Next to me on the drafting table was a military uniform.

"I'm sorry, my queen," the guard said when the door had closed. "Are you hurt?"

I pointed to the goo that still bound my mouth. I couldn't speak, and the guard realized that. He reached into a pouch on his belt and pulled out a handful of salt. He poured it over the good and it dissolved instantaneously, not even leaving a sticky residue as it disintegrated.

"My apologies, my queen," the guard said.

I furrowed my brow, slowly. "If I am your queen, why did you manhandle me so?"

"I had to make it look good for the others, but the Emerald soldiers will always be loyal to the true queen of Oz."

I raised my eyebrows. This was an interesting twist. "Oh, really? So, you will let me go, then?"

"Of course, your majesty. However, Boudica's guards will be on the lookout for anything suspicious. Put on this uniform, and you will be safe in our protection."

I knew I was a good witch, but that my spells still worked even after I lost my power was a welcome relief. I picked up a pair of bracers and placed them on my wrists. "And what of the false queen?"

"We work with your most loyal allies to thwart her. She will die before her coronation but, my queen, there is a problem."

"There are many problems," I grumbled. "What is it now?"

"The false queen has an ally in Queen Aine."

"The fairy queen? Ha. She *would* turn on me. She will be dealt with as well, in her time."

I expected as much. Queen Aine understood power better than anyone, and the moment she sniffed that Hypnos had anointed another, her allegiance shifted. I could not force the fairies to bow to me. They bowed because of what I offered them—a way out of Urgu—and when my power was taken from me, so was their allegiance. It didn't surprise me. Still, I would formulate a plan for her comeuppance later.

"Thank you, soldier. You will be rewarded when I am in power again. You will all be rewarded."

The soldier grabbed the chest plate and shoulder pauldrons and placed them over my head. "The gods' speed. When the final Mountain people come through the gate, there will be a distraction as the refugees look for their kin. At that time, go to the convoy and dive into the back of the last truck. Our people will be waiting for you."

I placed the helmet over my head. "You are a fine soldier, and your loyalty is commendable."

"There is one more thing, ma'am," he replied, averting his eyes.

"What is it?"

"You have to dust me."

"What?" I scoffed. "I'm not going to dust you."

He pulled a dagger from its sheath around his belt. "It's all been arranged. My partner is outside so that he can feign ignorance, but there are two guards who brought you here, and Boudica's troops know it. There cannot be three when we leave this place."

"No, soldier." I shook my head. "You are strong. You can withstand interrogation."

He placed the dagger in my hand. "We cannot take that risk. You are far too valuable. I have made my peace with the gods and go to them willingly."

I took a deep breath. There was no use arguing. My soldiers would protect my safety at all costs. While I could order him to stand down, there was clearly a plan in place, and I insulted his sacrifice to throw a wrench in them.

"Your sacrifice is honorable."

"I'm just happy I could do my part to protect you, my queen."

Without another word, I stuck the dagger through the soldier's throat. His eyes went wide, and he choked for a moment before exploding into dust and falling around the room and on my clothes.

I dropped the knife and opened the door. The lanky guard nodded to me as I passed, and when I walked across the grass, Boudica's men didn't look at me twice.

ROSE

"It's just up this way," the chef told me. We were both out of breath, having just ascended two flights of spiral stairs. Had I known how many stairs a castle had, and how often I would climb them, I might have just let myself die instead of taking Hypnos's blessing. I barely liked walking across campus, and I never worked out, so being queen was more exercise than I got just about...ever. I wasn't even getting any benefit from it, since I was pretty sure that souls didn't sweat.

The stairwell was lit with stained-glass windows every few feet. The glass was beautiful, with blues fading into reds and then mixing with yellows. I wished I lived there.

"This is one of the most beautiful hallways in the whole castle," I said, looking at the windows.

"You honor us, but it could not be nearly as ornate as your own bed chamber."

"You are wrong. My part of the castle is rather dark. Queen Nimue preferred blacks, and blotted out the windows, so I'm not sure how it would look with light streaming in everywhere."

The chef stopped in front of a door latched with a metal bar. "Well, you could just order them taken down."

I smiled. "Soon, I will. I have a lot on my mind."

"Of course. You are the queen."

"I have not had power long, and I often forget what I can and can't do."

The chef's mouth twitched. "May you have it for a long time."

"Thank you."

The chef banged the iron knocker on the wooden door. "Gwendolyn. Are you in there?" There was no answer. "Gwendolyn?" Again, nothing from inside. "I'm coming in."

The chef pushed up the bar and leaned against the door with all his might to open it, then beckoned me inside. I followed him into the room, which was as large as my own, with intricately crafted, gilded columns, beautiful hand-made chests, and a four-poster bed. I was jealous for a moment, until I remembered the reason for the fine accommodations was because food tasters were expected to die quickly.

"Oh my god!" the chef said, pointing to the bed. I rushed forward to see the food taster's ashes falling through the air and gathering in a fine dust on the bedspread. "And there!"

The chef pointed toward the wall, where, written in large black letters using soot, were the words "Long live the true queen" along with the image of a peacock.

"Nimue," I breathed.

I moved toward the sign and studied it closely. It was as if somebody had taken the ashes of Gwendolyn's body and sprawled it across the wall. "My word. What do you thin—"

But I couldn't finish my statement, because as I turned the chef lunged at me with a kitchen knife. "For the queen!"

"Stop!" I shouted, holding my hands out, and then, for a moment, he was frozen in place, unable to move, stuck in the air. "Oh right, I have powers. Duh. Nice of you to finally show yourself."

The chef tried to squirm away. "Let me go!"

"No!" I replied. "Why are you trying to kill me?"

"I serve the true queen of Oz."

"Ozma? She's dead."

"No, you daft girl. The true queen. Nimue!"

I couldn't control my laughter. I guffawed for a full thirty seconds as the chef gave me a puzzled look. When I finally subdued myself, I wiped the tears from my face and turned to him. "Nimue? You are willing to risk your life for her?"

"Of course. I pledged my soul to her."

"Hrm," I said. "Why?"

"She gave me everything. I was a poor farmer before she found me, and she gave me a job, a life, a wife, and status. There is not one person in the Emerald City that doesn't know who I am. They used to mock me. And now, without Nimue's protection, they do so again."

"I could have given you protection. Why don't you pledge your loyalty to me?"

"That's not how it works," the chef said with a sigh. "They feared Nimue."

"And what of me?"

His eyes locked with mine. "They don't think of you at all, except as a frightened child who doesn't understand power."

The words that dripped off his tongue angered me in a way that I hadn't been angry before. I was more than a child, and yet, even as the queen, I got as much respect as I had on the playgrounds back home.

"My queen!" I heard a gruff voice from the door. I turned my eyes to see the red-faced Balor, with his bushy beard and a bandaged arm, hobbling through the door. "Are you okay?"

I turned back to the chef. "As good as can be expected."

He hobbled forward. "I'm sorry I was detained. I went to the kitchen on Queen Aine's orders, but you weren't there."

"This is the best Red can do for protection, a crippled soldier?" I muttered to myself. "Wow, everybody really does hate me."

"There are few Red can trust. I promise you I am capable, though I fear I have let you down already."

I smiled a fake smile. "Think nothing of it. You are here and I am still safe." I turned back to the chef. "Go."

The chef tripped over his feet and scurried toward the door. Balor rushed across the room and picked him up with one hand, shaking him until the chef dropped the knife.

"What should I do with this one?" Balor asked.

"Put him in the dungeon until I figure out what to do with him, and if you can, find out who he works for."

"With extreme prejudice?" Balor asked.

I turned toward the door. "I don't want to know. I just want to know who he works for. Understood?"

As I turned out the door, I couldn't help but think that for the first time, I sounded almost queenly, and it took everything in my power to not jump for joy in the corridor, which would have ruined it. Instead, I just let a small smile creep across my face, a wave of satisfaction rolled over me.

CHAPTER 28
CHELLE

They're following me.

They tracked me all day and night.

Everywhere I went through the dark woods, they followed. Their yellow eyes crept closer. They would soon be on top of me, and I couldn't defeat them all.

In the distance a pair of purple eyes watched, waiting. What would happen then? *Will I be dusted? Can I be dusted? I have a body. Will it bleed? Will I die screaming?*

A cackle echoed in the distance. It was her. She could take me at any moment, but she didn't. *Why not?*

Because she loved the game. *What else did she have to fill an eternity?*

I clutched the golden book tightly in my hands. In the distance, neon. *Neon? Like a rave? Was there a rave in the woods?*

Who cares? There were people. There was light in the darkness, so I ran. The yellow-eyed shadows trailed close behind. A whoosh of air came upon me, and the back of my leg stung. I screamed. Blood rushed down my leg.

"*Lux!*" The sky filled with light. There was a shriek, and

the shadows retreated. I couldn't keep my hand in the air. The book was oblong, and awkward to carry, even though it was light. Too light. Even a gentle breeze rocked it from side to side.

I couldn't afford to drop it. When I drew my hand in to hold on to the book, the darkness fell again. All that was left for light were the eyes. I hightailed it toward the neon.

I broke through the clearing into the camp of fifty or so people. Dozens of ravers turned to me, except they weren't dancing. They simply milled around, cleaning their weapons and eating. When they turned to me, their eyes were bright and colored in the same neon as their hair. Their bodies were white as soap, and their clothes black.

When the screech sounded behind me, the ravers stood at the ready. "Shadow demons!" one of them shouted. The others gathered around me, chanting something I couldn't understand. The light from their hair and their eyes glowed more brilliantly. The disparate colors on their hair and eyes joined together and formed a white aura which exploded and cascaded into the woods.

The demons weren't just driven backward, they were torn apart by the light and destroyed. When it was over, a man with long dreadlocks and thick stubble reached down for me.

"What did you do to piss off the night queen?" he asked with a thick accent.

"Night queen?" I asked.

"Hera," a woman explained. Her eyes were a soft, glowing blue. "She controls the shadow demons and these woods. They do her bidding. Nasty buggers, but easy to deal with if you use the right spell."

I pulled myself to my feet. "How can you use magic? I thought there was no magic in Urgu."

"It is hard," the dreadlocked man said. "And we can only do so together, for each of us has just a tiny bit of magic bound inside us, keeping us alive."

"But I was told—"

"Forget what you were told. In Urgu, everything, even the currency of dreams, is bound with some magic. None of us can use magic on our own, but together, with deep concentration and teamwork, we can perform great deeds. The more of us there are, the more powerful it becomes. But it drains us quickly. We will have to regroup before we can use it again with any effectiveness. Let us hope we aren't attacked before then."

"That's amazing," I said. "Who are you—"

One of the Queen's Guard pushed through into the clearing. The others, recognizing his emerald peacock garment, grabbed their weapons. They were ready to fight but the soldier held up his hands.

"I mean you no harm. Your queen Boudica has bargained for your safe arrival into the Land of Oz. Come with me, and we will escort you to the Gates of Draongor."

I didn't know these people, but they could lead me back to Oz, and eventually, to Rose.

"Excuse me, may I come with you?" I asked the dreadlocked man as he moved to put out the fire burning in front of him.

"Well, you certainly can't stay here. Hera has her eyes on you. You will be safe in our protection, or at least safer than trying to get through these woods on your own."

CHAPTER 29

NIMUE

I crossed from the jail to the guard tower and into the refugee camp, careful to keep my gait slow and plodding, like the other guards. Although Boudica recognized me at first glance, I doubted her hayseed followers would be able to do the same. Most prisoners never made eye contact with guards, too frightened of the uniform to see them as anything but a symbol of their oppression. There was no doubt that the Mountain People were prisoners, but for semantics.

Night crept over the horizon. Soon it would fall on Oz as well. On the north side of the camp, the preparations for the caravan were nearly complete. At least a dozen soldiers worked tirelessly plotting my escape. Rose didn't know what she was playing at when she deposed my rule. My men were still loyal to me. They would always be loyal to me, and soon, I would be back on the throne of Oz—with or without my powers.

The Mountain People wandered about the camp. Soon the rest of their clan would enter through the gates, and I would use the distraction to make my exit. I flicked my fingers, trying to make a flame inside of them like I had so many hundreds of times in the past. The Mountain People had rudimentary magic that was once laughable to me, but I would kill for some of it now.

"Excuse me?" A young girl stood in front of me.

I froze, fearing she had recognized me. "Yes?"

"Are you a guard?" she asked, sitting down next to me.

"Why, yes I am."

The girl squinted at my face, though I was making a point not to look at her. "I've never seen you before."

I grunted. "I've never seen you, either."

"Well, I've been here for a long time."

"I have not." I tilted my head down slowly, aware of the girl's purple eyes studying me. "I am new."

"Why have you come all the way to the Gates?" she asked, pulling out a block of wood and a knife and began to whittle. "Nobody likes being stationed here."

"Why not?"

The girl studied the block of wood. "It's so boring."

"Is that so? And the guards told you they didn't like it here?"

She shook her head. "No, but I hear things. Guards talk. They think we're invisible, but we're not. So, did you do something bad to end up here?"

"No," I shook my head. "I've come to protect you, like we all have. We have sworn to protect you and the other Mountain People."

A sad smile creased on her pale face. "Oh, then you don't know?"

"Know what, my child?"

"There are no mountain people anymore. At least, not out there, 'cept for a few dozen like my parents who are coming in tonight. We got driven from the Mountains some time ago."

I feigned horror. "I have heard, but you are strong. You will persist."

"Not strong enough for what's coming for us."

"What's coming?"

The girl shook her head. "Mama won't tell me, but she says it's bad. In those last weeks before we left, almost our whole village died. It wasn't 'til Boudica drove the monsters out and bought us some time that we could flee. Children first, then our parents. We didn't want to leave. We were the last town left on the hill. But we couldn't stay. Not sure anybody can stay in the mountains."

"But Agrona should protect you, as she always has."

Agrona was a Celtic war goddess that was banished to Urgu for her bloodlust. She took refuge in the mountains when no other deity wanted it. The winters were harsh, and the people were savage. The monsters were dangerous, even for the gods, but Agrona took to it up there. When she signed her peace treaty with the other gods, she requested the mountains—demanded them, actually. She never gave her blessing to any mortal, and only wished to be left alone, atop the tallest mountain.

"Agrona is cruel and mean," the girl said. "She has abandoned us. There was a time we could pray to her, and she would protect us, but those days were long before I came to Urgu."

"How long have you been here?" I asked.

"A hundred and thirty-two years, give or take."

"Not long before the dreamers stopped coming," I said. "And your mother and father came, too. That's unusual."

She shook her head. "They aren't really my mom and dad, but they took me in when I showed up, and I've been with them longer than my own parents. They kept me safe in the Mountains. Most people think it's a curse to enter the Dream Realm up there, but I thought it was a blessing. I found family. They kept me safe. We stayed strong. People left us alone. 'Course, now it's different up there."

I wondered vaguely what was happening in the Mountains but didn't really care. I was entranced by the idea the small child had given me. Nobody had ever received Agrona's blessing before, meaning her power would be strong, maybe stronger than any other god. If I were to find Agrona, perhaps she would bestow her blessing on me, and then I could retake Urgu in her name. I just had to find a way to reach her without being ripped in half by the beasts that roamed the Mountains.

"You are here," I heard a woman say behind me. "Good."

A young woman with the milkiest skin I had ever seen came toward me. She moved slowly, and I realized as she neared that her skin was not just white, but made of ceramic, mixed in with clear glass. A dark cloud like a smoke storm billowing behind it. The little girl gathered up her whittling and was gone, running halfway across the camp in the time it took the porcelain woman to come to a stop in front of me. "The soothsayer will see you now," she said.

I shook my head. "I never asked to see a Soothsayer."

"She is very interested in meeting you. You would not want to keep her waiting."

I had heard of the Soothsayer. She cheated death and transformed herself into a living monument to eternal life, and she did it all after being dusted. While the others in the Mountain People could only use magic by themselves, the soothsayer was magic down to her very essence.

The Mountain People protected her over all else, and every time we tried to abduct her for our own study, none of our men would survive. We lived in an uneasy alliance, allowing her to remain in Oz with her people, hoping one day for an audience with her to learn what she knew.

Today was the day. I had my chance, and though I feared it was a trap, I couldn't deny her. I pushed myself up and brushed myself off.

"Very well," I said. "Lead the way."

CHAPTER 30
RED

Night had fallen by the time we finished with the watch commander. I said my goodbyes to Boudica and walked toward the jail cell where I would find Nimue, hopefully sniveling. I desperately wanted to see her cry.

The guards were prepping a caravan to go north, which I thought odd since there were barely enough guards at the gates as it was, but far be it from me to get involved in military matters. I just wanted to get Nimue back to the Emerald City. Without the fairies for help, it would take a week to make it to Oz, and I had no interest in waiting any longer than necessary to leave.

A single guard was stationed outside the door to the jail. She must really be weakened. She was no longer a sorcerer, that was for sure. After all, Boudica brought her through the gates in a wheelbarrow.

I nodded to the guard, and he opened the door to let me inside. I was looking forward to seeing Nimue in her decrepit state, but the jail cell was empty save for a knife and a pile of black ash, no doubt the remnants of another guard. The knife was inlaid with the peacock crest of Hera.

I rushed out of the room. "Did you see Nimue run out of here?"

The guard looked bewildered. "N-n-n-no, ma'am. I thought—"

Useless. I didn't even wait for him to finish. There were only two possibilities; either Nimue stole a guard's clothing and ran off, or she was given a set of clothes and the guards helped her escape. Either was equally likely, and in both cases the guard at the door was useless.

I knelt to the ground and found a boot print that resembled the one the guard used. That meant they were everywhere in the camp, and there was no way to track a single boot print. If Nimue had disappeared into the woods, it would take days to find her. If the guards were helping her, I had a good sense that the caravan heading north was being set up for her. It hadn't left yet, which meant I still had a chance to find her.

But if she was still here, where would she be? There were not many places to hide in the barracks, especially not for somebody of Nimue's stature. The most logical place to hide was the refugee camp. There were few people who would recognize her there, save for Boudica and her troops, and most likely the refugees would not recognize her in uniform. It was as good a place as any to start, so I made my way toward it.

The night brought out the Mountain People, who were beginning to cook and perform their duties around the camp, from washing clothing to mending their tents. I headed for the soothsayer's tent.

"Are you looking for the lady guard?" a young girl with light purple eyes asked me. She was whittling a small block of wood.

"I don't know," I said with a shrug. "Is she new here?"

"I've never seen her before, and I've seen everybody before, y'know? Kind of the curse of a long life."

She looked young, but that meant very little in Urgu. "Where did she go?"

"With Shaina," she replied, pointing to the soothsayer's tent. "They went into her tent a while ago and haven't been out since. I hope they didn't kill her. That lady was nice, even for a guard."

I chuckled. "I promise you, nice is not the right word to describe that one, if she is who I believe her to be."

"Everybody's nice in their own way," the girl said, turning back to her whittling, and taking a cut out of a piece of bark.

I watched her whittling for a moment before I asked, "What's that going to be?"

"I dunno," she replied. "Smaller, I reckon."

"Fair enough." I turned away from her toward the tent. Shaina had exited and was holding her hand out to me.

"You may not attack when you enter," she said. "This tent is a place of peace."

"So, you didn't kill her?" I asked.

"Of course not."

A look of consternation fell over my face. "Then why is she still here?"

If she could move her face, Shaina would have smiled. I was sure of it, because a slight titter escaped her lips. "We're waiting for you, of course."

"Nimue is waiting for me? I find that unlikely."

Shaina shook her head, but it was more like she shook her whole body from side to side, and her head was an ancillary byproduct of her body moving. "It is true. She has a purpose, and you will help her fulfill it."

This time, I laughed. "I highly doubt that."

"You may see for yourself." Shaina gestured toward the tent. "Do you agree not to attack inside the tent?"

I nodded. "If Nimue's not aggressive, then I have no reason to be."

"Wonderful." Shaina moved aside and held open the flap of the tent for me. I ducked my head inside, gripping the hilts of my daggers, ready to fight, but hoping I could hold to my promise. Inside, Nimue sat across from the soothsayer drinking a cup of tea. When she saw me, she smiled.

"There you are," Nimue said. Her voice was soft. "Right on time."

"I am...vexed by your pleasant greeting."

"Why would she not greet you kindly?" the soothsayer said. "She has a great destiny, and you are part of it."

"Her destiny is getting dusted in the Emerald City, which will be great, but not for her."

Nimue placed the tea down and stood up. "You are very morbid. Did you know that?"

I let go of my daggers. "And you are quite chipper for one who is under arrest by the crown."

"Here now. I can just appreciate irony. After all, a month ago I was out for your head, and now, you are out for mine."

"You do understand all we talked about?" the soothsayer asked in a dour tone. "And that if you say anything to anyone, you damage your chances of it coming true."

Nimue nodded. "I do."

"Then go with the gods. May they treat you better than they have treated us."

I grabbed Nimue by the cuff of her cloak. "Enough of this. Every moment we wait is another we waste back to the Emerald City."

Nimue didn't take her eyes off of the soothsayer. "Oh, we're not going back to the Emerald City. Not yet at least."

"And why not?" I scoffed. "You do not control our travel schedule."

"Because if we do, your friend Chelle, and everyone outside the gates, will be dead by morning. We must go to them."

I pushed open the flap to the tent. "Since when do you care about anybody besides yourself?"

"Since I must," Nimue said, looking back again at the soothsayer before I pushed her out the door.

"I hope our paths do not cross again," I said to the shrouded woman.

"They will," the soothsayer spoke in a rasping voice. "When the time is right. Do not forget about me."

"I don't think that could ever happen," I replied, then headed outside. Magic put me ill at ease and even the soothsayer's gentle words were not enough to stop my hair from standing on edge. At least now that I had apprehended Nimue, my travels had not been in vain.

If I could not save Chelle, though, I couldn't shake the feeling that I would be a failure, and rightfully dusted by our new queen.

CHAPTER 31

ROSE

"I'm just saying we should murder them all," Queen Aine said as we descended the spiral stairs to the dungeon. The smell of stale bread and cooked cabbage filled the air, and the cool air licked my skin.

"We're not going to murder them," I replied. "Besides, I'm very sure that when a queen kills someone, it's not called murder."

"That is true. Still, I think we should dust them all. This is the third attempt in as many days. That's a lot, in case you didn't know, not being royalty and all."

"There will be a coronation soon, and then, I will be officially queen, and everything will be better."

"Wow. You really are naïve."

I reached the bottom of the stairwell. "I've heard that before."

I'd heard it throughout my whole life, but I wasn't naïve. I just refused to see the worst in people. People had always been pretty horrible to me, from my parents, to my boyfriends, to my teachers, to...literally everybody but Chelle, so thinking the best about people allowed me to function in a world that had pretty much wanted me dead since I was born.

Back on Earth, I was diabetic and poor. I didn't have health insurance, so it was literally like my own government was trying to kill me by charging me $700 a month for insulin. I might not have been struggling against bounty hunters like Chelle, but I was constantly fighting death dealing with people pretending to have my best interests at heart. It wasn't much different having everybody trying to kill me in Urgu.

"These people are rotten, my dear," Queen Aine said. "You need to replace them."

"People are not rotten," I replied. "They just don't know me. Once they know me, they will love me."

That had never been true, except for once, in my entire life, but I couldn't stop trying. If I stopped trying, then what was the point in anything? I should just dust myself right now if I believed I couldn't change people's opinions of me.

God, that actually sounded nice. Dusting myself. Not having to worry about any of this at all. Succumbing to the slings and arrows and vanishing in a cloud of dust. Ozma didn't have to deal with this stuff anymore. She was a cloud of dust. Yeah, she no longer existed, but she also didn't have to deal with people constantly trying to kill her, either, or the ridiculous questions posed to her every minute of every day.

As nice as that sounded, I wanted to live. *Stupid will.* And I wanted to see Chelle again, even though she ripped my heart out for leaving me. *Stupid love.*

"Aye," Balor's voice boomed down the hall. "That is a bonny dish. I love a good cabbage stew."

I expected Balor to be wailing on the little chef, breaking every bone in his body, assuming souls still had bones, but instead he was tipping his chair back, drinking some mead, resting his feet on the cell bars.

"What's going on here?" I asked. "This does not seem like an interrogation to me."

Balor hopped to his feet. "Nay, queen. He doesn't seem to know anything, though. I gave him a right good thrashing, and he swore up and down he worked on his own."

"I don't believe him." I turned to the chef, stone-faced. "Nimue has been deposed and exiled. I saw to it myself. She's never coming back."

The chef and Balor looked at each other, then laughed. The chef turned back to me, leaning into the light and I saw that his face had been worked over like tenderized meat.

"That's rich." The chef wiped his nose with the back of his hand. "The queen ruled Oz for over a hundred years. Her alliances run thick. Who do you have? You might trust the Unseelie garbage hovering next to you, but you don't know what I know about her. She is cold hearted. She will turn on you in a second."

"Do you think I don't know that?"

The chef smiled. "No. I don't think you know much of anything, princess."

I wanted to scream. I wanted to rage. I had done everything for Urgu. I risked my life on Earth for it, and nobody respected me even one iota.

"Queen!" I roared. "You will address me as queen."

"Why? Either way I'm bound for dusting."

I stepped forward, rage filling my lungs. "Then, why wait?"

"Queen," Queen Aine said. "No. This is merely a traitor, and a low rung one at that. Keeping him alive will ferret out the others."

I wheeled on her. "What does it matter? Like you said,

we should kill them all, and maybe, just maybe, you're right."

Queen Aine gulped loudly. "Well, yeah, I suppose I could be right about that."

"Or maybe it's you." My eyes narrowed. "The attacks did not start until you showed up here, after all."

"That's preposterous. I made a deal with your paramour to keep you safe."

"Yes, until she returned. And where is Chelle? Where is she?"

"I don't know!" Queen Aine screamed. "She was given to Hera to get her into—"

"Hera!" I shouted. "You gave her to Hera?"

"The only way to get her into the castle was as a gift to the goddess. With any luck, she'll be on her way back here."

Chelle. I had been so wrapped up in finding my murderers that I had forgotten all about her for a moment. *Chelle.*

The necklace.

I gave her the necklace, and I could go to her and see her to make sure she was okay. If she wasn't, there would be Hell to pay in the Emerald City. I could barely stand the thought of Chelle leaving by her own will, but the thought of her being corrupted by Hera, or, worse, killed by her, filled me with fear and rage.

"You," I said to Queen Aine. "Come with me. We will see where Chelle is, and if she's hurt, then you will be the first to be dusted."

"You can't threaten me!"

I balled my hands into fists. Fire filled them without me even thinking about it, and the flames came out of my eyes. The fire licked my face, but it didn't burn. The heat felt good upon my skin. "Do not speak to me like a child. You yourself said I needed a show of force, and if that means destroying every Unseelie in the Enchanted Woods and burning it to the ground, then maybe people will fear me. Maybe the Emerald City is incapable of love. Maybe all they have left is fear, and if Chelle is gone, then it is all I have left inside of me, too, so you had better hope that nothing happened to her."

I took a deep breath and felt myself cool by several dozen degrees as I turned back to the chef.

"She's pissed," the chef murmured to Balor, who was looking at me with wide-eyed horror.

"And you," I said, stomping over to the chef's cell. "Are you very sure you know nothing about the conspiracy to end my life?"

The chef gulped. "I am very sure."

I leaned into the bars. "Then what good are you?" I raised my hand into the air. With every inch I raised it, the little chef hovered higher into the air, his legs thrashing in the air as he struggled to breath. I clasped my hands together and the chef exploded into a million pieces. When I spun around, both Queen Aine and Balor stared at me, mouths agape.

"I can't believe—" Balor said, barely able to speak. "Why?"

I didn't have to answer him, or anyone. I was the queen, and as the queen, I was free to do as I liked, and I very much liked that idea.

"Do you serve at my pleasure?" I asked.

He nodded. "I do, ma'am."

"And you are loyal to me?"

"I am."

"Then stop asking questions," I scowled, before moving toward the stairwell. "Come with me, Queen Aine. The fate of your people hangs in the balance. Let us see the depths of your betrayal."

I didn't know what came over me, but for the second time in the day, I felt like a queen; a wicked queen no doubt, but a queen no less. I would have my way, and if Chelle was dead, there would be blood and vengeance, the type that fairy kind would never recover from.

CHAPTER 32

NIMUE

"Ow!" I shouted as Red led me behind her horse toward the Gates of Droangor. I could barely keep up with the horse at a trot, let alone a gallop, and was being half-dragged as she forced me from the refugee camp toward the watch commander's office. "Can you please wait for me?"

"You should get used to this," Red replied. "It will be this way until we reach the Emerald City."

She pulled up the reins in front of the watch commander's office and I slid to a stop. I pushed myself up and brushed myself off. "Thank you."

"This is not a courtesy," Red replied. "I have business to attend to before we get on our way. Wait here. Then, we will not stop again until reaching Chelle."

Red hopped off her horse and whispered to Boudica's men, who were milling around the watch commander's office. After a moment, they nodded, and she disappeared inside. The men gathered around me, snarling, no doubt aware of the conspiracy to free me.

I plopped down on the dirt and crossed my legs. According to the Soothsayer, if I were to help Chelle get

back to Rose and be a welcome witness to Rose's coronation, I would be able to open the Obsidian Spindle and
return to Earth. However, I had to join the resistance willingly, and work to help it grow, or I would be slaughtered
before the end of my first night in captivity.

The last part was the only part I wholeheartedly
believed, given how much Red hated me, but it's hard to
argue with a floating ball of ash contained in a porcelain
body. The soothsayer was very convincing. The only way
out was through, and though it turned every knot in my
stomach, I knew she was right.

"Damn it!" Red said, walking out of the building.

"What is it, dear?" I asked.

"Not that you care, but they won't open the gates to me,
or to anyone, until Boudica's people show up. But they
won't show up because they'll be ambushed and killed
before they make it here."

I pushed myself to my feet. "Oh, is that all? I can help
with that."

"Yes," Red sneered, "I'm sure you can convince your
conniving guards to open the door for you."

"Well, yes, I might be able to do that, too, but I was
thinking of another way. A way my men used to leave Oz
when I needed them to conduct secret business."

"And what way is this?"

"Give me a horse and I will show you."

Red laughed.

"Look, I know I'm going to die when I get to the
Emerald City. I know you need to rescue your friend before
we get there, so I have every reason to delay your plans, and
yet, I am helping you willingly. All I ask is that you give me
the courtesy of treating me like a human being. Is that so
much?"

"Yes," Red snarled. "But what choice do I have?"

"You could let them all die."

Red leapt onto her horse. "Hop on."

We rode for two hours into the woods bordering the encampment. There was little moonlight except what came through the trees. Eventually, the trail became too narrow for us to ride. Red helped me down, since I was tied up, and we continued on by foot. She led me along with a rope.

"You had better not be lying to me."

"Yes, you've mentioned that," I replied. "Your threats have become stale. I am a deposed, magicless, much hated woman in Oz, possibly the most hated in all Urgu. If you dusted me, you would be doing me a favor."

Red yanked the rope. "You won't get off so easily."

As we walked deeper into the woods, the faint light of the moon was replaced by a bright glow. "Ah, yes, here we are."

We walked into a clearing with a bright red tree in its center. The lonely tree, gnarled at the root and twisted at the branches, glowed as if it were on fire from the inside.

"What is this?"

"Portals, my dear. I created them all around Urgu for quick travel. Magic travel is so dreadfully annoying, as you know, with the headaches and the dizziness. Besides, as a queen I couldn't be bothered to handle the transport of all my many spies, so they used these to travel."

"This is why I could never find them."

"Honestly, I'm surprised Ozma never found them. I thought she was so bright, and there are so many of them around Oz. We were barely trying to hide it."

I yanked the rope holding me as I moved forward, and Red tumbled after me. The tree was cool to my touch as I ran my hand around the back of it until I found a gnarled knot. "There we are."

I pushed into the knot and out popped a knob. "Let's see, I believe we need number twenty-four. I looked around in the tree bark until I found a knobby dial numbered from one to fifty. I turned it until the glowing yellow notch on the top of the knot aligned with 24. "There we are."

The hole at the front of the tree began to glow a soft yellow from its dark red.

"What do we do now?" Red asked.

I gestured toward the tree. "Now, you walk inside."

"Yeah, right. Like I'm going to trust you. You first."

"Seriously?" I asked, rolling my eyes. "I'm trying to help you."

"Then prove it." Red held tight to the rope. "If you try anything funny, I'll choke you."

"Easy, darling. Save that for later."

I stepped up to the portal and took a deep breath. If I chose correctly, then I would be in the dark woods again, near Hera's castle. If I chose poorly, I could be anywhere in Urgu. I turned back toward Red one time and gave her a smile which went unreturned.

"See you on the other side."

I stepped through the portal and disappeared into the yellow light.

CHAPTER 33
CHELLE

You can't possibly escape me.

I am everywhere.

I am eternal.

Hera's voice pounded in my head most of the long night, slowing my gait and forcing me back from the rest of the Mountain People as we neared the Gates of Droangor.

I have only let you live this long for my own amusement.

Hoping you would change your mind.

Hoping you would choose me over that foolish girl.

"I don't understand," I mumbled. "I'm trying to open the Obsidian Spindle. I'm trying to find a way back to Earth. Don't you want that?"

I want you to follow my orders. I want you to give your free will to me, and that you choose to defy me still...causes me grave concern.

"I will never follow you."

I know.

It's a pity that all these people must die in order for you to learn your lesson.

"No, please."

You could have prevented this.

The shrieks rang through the forest. Not just in front of me, but behind and on all sides. They were everywhere.

"Form up!" one of the Mountain People shouted, and they all formed a protective circle around me.

"We only have one shot at this!" said another.

"Do we even have one?" another screamed. "I'm still weak from the last time."

"We have to try!" growled a low voice.

We were so close to the Gates, and safety, and now, they would all die for protecting me.

"*LUX!*" I shouted, and a thousand pairs of eyes reflected the light from my hands.

"Now!" The gravelly-voiced man shouted, and a thousand colors molded into one beam of white light and cascaded across the forest. When it was done, I looked up. For a moment, there was darkness, and then, the eyes came back, with Hera's purple ones glowing behind them.

Did you really think that would work a second time? How foolish do you think I am?

I dropped to my knees as the sound of her voice pierced my head. In the surrounding woods, a low-pitched growl turned into a high-pitched shrill scream. I nearly didn't see the attack begin, for the shadow demons moved in the darkness.

"*LUX!*" I shouted, and the light flew into the air once more. "*LUX!*"

The demons fell just out of reach of my light. I couldn't keep it up for long. I was dreadfully tired from casting so many spells, and each one was less powerful than the one that came before it.

A pity that you will not live to see the destruction of the Emerald City. I look forward to dusting your girlfriend personally.

"No!" I screamed.

Yes, and there is nothing you can do about it, because you are pitiful.

As I fought to hold back Hera's voice torturing on my mind, a familiar figure rushed toward me.

"Red?" I whispered.

She gripped a rope in her hand and pulled someone along at the end of it. Their bodies whipped through the shadow demons chasing after them.

"Don't worry," she replied with a nod. "We're here."

Red joined the Mountain People encircling me, as the woman she carried dropped to her knees and I caught a glimpse of her face.

"Nimue?"

"Ah, good. You remember me."

"I hate you," I snarled.

"Hate me later," Nimue replied with a dismissive tone. "For now, you need to speak this spell to banish Hera from your head."

"I would never do anything for you."

"Do it!" Red said. "Otherwise, we'll all die."

"Yes," I muttered.

"Good," Nimue replied. "Then say, 'Be gone cow-eyed god. Leave me be.'"

No!

"Say it!" Nimue shouted.

I wasn't powerful enough to perform spells in English. No matter how hard I tried, I was never able to master it. "Latin. I need Latin."

"No, you don't! Just say it."

"Be gone...cow-eyed god. Leave me be." Nothing happened. "See! I told you."

"You're lying to yourself. The reason Latin works is because you believe it will work. Now, BELIEVE!"

I fell onto the ground as the shriek drowned out everything else. "Be gone, cow-eyed god. Leave me be. BE GONE, COW-EYED GOD. LEAVE ME BE!"

"AGAIN!"

"BE GONE, COW-EYED GOD. LEAVE ME BE!"

"With feeling!"

"BE GONE, COW-EYED GOD. LEAVE ME BE!"

There was a thundering sound beneath me, and a crack of lightning sounded in the distance, and then, the ringing stopped.

"How do you feel?" Nimue asked.

A shiver ran through my spine. "A bit better."

Nimue unlatched my hand from the book I'd stolen from Hera and lifted it into the air. "Good, now you have to hold that light up above you while we get you to freedom."

"I can't. The book."

"Give it to me," Nimue said.

"Fat chance," I scoffed.

"I'll hold it," Red replied, placing two daggers into her belt. "Not like my daggers will do much good anyway against these beasts."

I nodded and handed the book to Red. "Don't lose it."

Nimue helped me to my feet. "Good, now you have to hold the light around all of us."

I shook my head. "It's too much."

"I know it's a lot, and Hera has drained much of your power, but if you don't, we'll all die."

I was weakened from fighting Hera in my head, but I nodded slowly. "I'll try."

Nimue shook her head. "I'm afraid that won't be enough. I need you to do it."

I chuckled. "That's funny."

"I don't get it."

I let out another meek laugh. "That is why you fail."

The shrieks of the shadow demons spread through the woods. Nimue's head snapped toward the origin of the sound. "They're coming."

"Now!" Nimue shouted.

"*LUX!*" I shouted, holding both my hands up into the air. The light that came from them was brighter than anything I ever conjured before, and it was nearly impossible to hold it together in my weakened state. "I can't—"

"Yes, you can!" Nimue said. "Follow me."

She led us through the woods, with Red behind her holding her leash. I could barely keep my eyes open, and my arms and legs were like jelly, but I struggled against my body's will to sleep. The light coursed around the group as we moved in a pack.

Up ahead I saw a tree that looked like it was burning embers from the inside. Nimue ran to it and rubbed her hand along its bark. A moment later, the red of the tree turned into a yellow glow.

"Inside!" Red shouted, and the group rushed toward the tree. I was the last to go, standing on the edge with just Nimue and Red.

"Come on," Red said, grabbing my arm.

The light faded as I let down my arms, but then there was something else glowing. My broach was giving off a faint light.

Rose.

"Rose?" I said, breathlessly, as I fell backwards into the tree and disappeared. The shadow demons fell in on me, but I was safe. I knew I was safe because I had Rose, and because Red was with me, and I allowed those two thoughts to carry me into the light as I faded out of consciousness.

CHAPTER 34

ROSE

The mirror turned to white, and then went dead, and my heart skipped a beat.

"Are you happy now?" Queen Aine asked. "She's fine."

"She is not fine," I replied. "She is not fine at all!"

"You're right. She's not," Queen Aine replied. "But she's *not* with Hera, and if you noticed, Red has the book they were searching for, and Nimue, meaning they should be back soon, just like I promised. As I said, I'm on your side. I've always been on your side."

I sat down on a plush couch next to the mirror. "Well, not always. You did try to kill me once."

"Yes, yes, but that is all in the past, just like your outburst at me in the dungeon. It's all water under the bridge, yes?"

I pushed myself to my feet. "I should have you hanged. I could do it, you know!"

"Please," Queen Aine said. "I've been trying to get you to kill those traitors in your small council for days, and you've done nothing. You really think you can be this cruel queen? Do you really think you can play that part?"

"I can and I will!" I screamed. "I killed that baker back in the dungeon, and I don't even feel bad about it!" Oh my god. I really didn't feel bad about it. How could I not feel bad about it? As I stared at Queen Aine, my lip began to quiver, and tears filled my eyes. "I'm exactly the monster you taught me to be, and you should fear that."

"Then do it," Queen Aine scowled. "If you think I should die, then come kill me." She held out her arms. "I won't even put up a fight."

I opened my mouth to scream for my guards, but nothing came out. My lip trembled as I looked at Queen Aine. She had betrayed me. She deserved to die. But she wasn't some baker that I didn't know from Adam. She was my friend, my companion. She was the only person who helped me when everybody else, even my own girlfriend, turned away from me.

Queen Aine fluttered over to me and placed herself on my shoulder. "It's okay."

The moment her feet touched my shoulder, I began to cry. "I killed that poor baker. Did you see that I killed him, without a second thought? How could I do that?"

"Your emotions got the best of you," Queen Aine said. "It happens."

"I don't know," I replied. "I felt like I was in complete control, maybe for the first time in my whole life. It didn't feel like me, but it felt exactly like me at the same time."

Queen Aine let out a deep sigh. "You have to be hard, sometimes, Rose. That's what it means to be queen, but you also have to know when to be soft, and compassionate. I am very good at the first thing, and bad at the second thing, whereas, you are very good at the second part. Together, we are almost one functional queen."

"Almost," I chuckled as I wiped the tears from my eyes.

"Can I please be forgiven now? I know I don't deserve it, but I would very much like not to die."

I looked up at her. "I suppose so, but if anything happens to Chelle..." My face dropped. "I don't know what I will do."

"Fair enough. Then I shall help hasten her return." Queen Aine floated off my shoulder. "I will send one of my men down to fetch them as soon as possible, but we have another matter to discuss, mainly, the attempts on your life, and getting you to your coronation."

Who could think of a coronation at a time like this? "I don't even care about the coronation. I just want to see Chelle again."

"I understand that, and I promise to reunite the both of you, but the coronation is in two days, and if we don't ferret out the assassination plot before then, well, you might have the shortest reign in Urgu's history. Is that what you want?"

I shook my head.

"I should hope not."

I frowned, thinking that I had never read about the reigns of the queens in the books I had looked over in my studies. "Out of curiosity, what is the shortest reign?"

Queen Aine closed her eyes, thinking. "Currently, the shortest reign is three days, so let us at least beat that, yes?"

I flopped back into my chair. "I don't want to deal with any of this. How did it get so hard?"

"It became hard when you became queen. There is a lot to being a...nothing burger, was that what you call it?"

I pushed myself to my feet. "Once Nimue comes back here, the assassins and conspirators will stop at nothing to return her to the throne."

Queen Aine nodded. "That is why I think you should kill them all."

"Maybe you're right." I buried my head in my hands. "I don't know. I don't know what to do."

"How did it feel to kill that chef?"

I sighed. "Horrible. It felt absolutely horrible."

Queen Aine stared at me for a moment, trying to figure out if I was lying to her or not, but eventually, she turned away. "Understandable that you didn't like it, but it brought you some fear among everyone in this castle. You showed them you have the stones to take someone's life, and that will not be taken lightly in Oz."

"How many people do you think hate me?"

Queen Aine chuckled. "Oh, my dear. They don't hate you. They just love power, and Nimue gave it to them."

I pulled my head out of my hands. "And I can take it away."

"Exactly."

"Or I could kill them."

Queen Aine nodded. "Yes."

I shrugged. "Or I could do nothing."

"Not what I would recommend, but yes, that is also possible."

I pushed myself to my feet. "Can you please call a small council meeting? I would like to look my enemies in the eye before I decide what to do with them."

Queen Aine floated up to meet me. "I don't think that's wise. Seeing them as human will prevent you from making the hard decisions that need to be made."

"Possibly, but most of my reign has been filled with unwise things, so what is another one? Please, Aine. I'm asking you, not ordering you, but I can order you if you would prefer."

Queen Aine dropped her head. "Yes, your majesty. It will be done."

I smiled at her. "Thank you." I had no idea what I would say to the small council, but by the end I would know if they would be dusted, exiled, or continue serving at my pleasure.

What I wanted more than anything was to see Chelle again. She always knew what to do, but I feared that she would convince me to kill all my enemies, and I wasn't prepared to have blood on my hands—or ash, as the case may be, in Urgu.

Am I dead?

Those were the first words that popped in my head when I came back into consciousness. It took me a moment to remember that I was in Urgu, in the Dream Realm, and that while I was not dead, everybody around me was dead, with the exception of Rose. Assuming she wasn't dead.

Rose.

I could finally go home to here and bring her the book—
The book!

Where was the book?

I struggled to focus my vision and when I finally did, I realized I was resting in a hammock inside an ornate and lavish tent. There were voices all around me. First Nimue, then one I hadn't ever heard before. I looked over and nearly did a double take. Nimue sat on an oriental carpet speaking with a woman...who wasn't quite a woman. Her face was covered in porcelain and glass.

Wait.

No.

She wasn't covered in it. Her face was made of porcelain

and glass. Behind it, a black cloud of ash bubbled and swirled like a tornado.

"What happened?" I said, my voice hoarse.

The porcelain woman looked over at me slowly, and her bright eyes seemed to look through me. "Oh good. You're up."

Between them I saw the golden book I had stolen from Hera, lying open, lit by candles on either side.

"Hey!" I shouted, falling off the hammock. "Get away from that book."

"Easy," Nimue said, holding up her arms. "The sooth-sayer doesn't like violent movements, being as delicate as she is."

"I don't care," I said, crawling forward. "Give me the book."

The woman held up her black, porcelain hands, slowly. "You may have it, but please, be gentle."

Nimue closed the book and handed it to me. "Not like we learned anything. It's just a bunch of blank pages."

"I know that," I replied, cradling the book. "Only the one blessed by Hypnos can read it, which is why I'm bringing it to Rose."

"Of course," Nimue said with a smile. "You have access to Rose, and she will be able to read it. Do you think she will, though?"

"Yeah," I said, glaring at her. "We're going home and we're going to be happy."

"I know you say that," Nimue replied in a somber tone. "But Rose is a queen here. Back at home, she's...not. I know something about power, and how it...as they say, corrupts absolutely."

"She's not like that," I said. "She's a bit confused now,

but she's going to come around. Once I get back, I'll show her that we have to go home."

"I hope you do," the soothsayer said in rhythmic cadence. "I would give anything to return to Earth. Literally anything."

"Amen to that," Nimue chimed in.

I pushed myself to my feet. "And that is why Rose must see reason. If she stayed behind, it would be an affront to everybody in Urgu. She has to understand that much. Everybody will hate her when they learn what she gave up to be here."

"It's not unclear that everybody doesn't hate her now," Nimue replied with a grim smile.

Red walked into the tent carrying my locket. It cast a blue light on her face. "Yes, my queen. We will come back as soon as we can."

"My locket!" I shouted. "Would you people quit stealing from me?"

Red rolled her eyes. "Chelle is a bit dramatic."

"Yes, she is," Rose said through the glass, and I nearly dropped the book on the ground at the sound of her voice.

"Rose?" I said, walking over to the necklace. Red held it up for me as I cradled the golden book in my hands. There she was, beautiful as always, smiling at me.

"Hi, Chelle. I miss you."

Tears filled my eyes. "I miss you too, baby. We're coming home soon."

"I know," Rose said with a kind smile. "Queen Aine's fairies should be there to take you home any moment."

"Queen Aine is a traitor! She sold me to Hera for—"

Rose held up her hand. "I know what she did, and we've talked about it."

"Talked about it!" I shouted. "Do you know—"

"She says she did it to save you. She wanted to get you into Hera's castle so you could steal the book without having to break in yourself. The book? Do you have it?"

I held it up for her to see. "I got it."

"And Nimue?"

Red turned the locket over to show Nimue. "She is in our custody."

"You have her, too." Rose sighed. "Then, as much as I abhor Aine's methods, they seem to have been successful."

"I suppose," I grumbled.

"Please come back soon. I would hate for you to miss my coronation."

"Yes, Rose, about that. With the book, we can go home and—"

Rose's eyes dropped and she shook her head vigorously. "Not now. Let's talk about that when you get here. A lot has happened since you've been gone."

"I'll see you soon," I said, brushing my hand against the locket as Rose faded from view.

"You know you can't go back, right?" Red said.

"What do you mean?" I asked, indignant.

"Queen Aine made a deal to protect Rose until you returned. The minute you step foot back in that castle, she will have fulfilled your bargain and whatever nefarious plan the fairy sees fit to carry out, she will be free to do so."

I hadn't thought of that. "Oh my god, you're right."

"Give the book to me," Red said, holding out her hand. "I will share it with Rose, and when we have a plan, I will call you back."

"Do I have to?"

"Only if you want Rose to live," Red said, matter-of-fact.

I handed Red the book, and she gave me the locket. "I hate this plan," I said.

"Yes, but you are known for being headstrong and fool-hardy. Perhaps if we show some restraint, we can keep Rose safe for a while longer."

I cast a wry smile. "And throw a wrench into the queen's plans, whatever they are."

Another woman with porcelain and glass for skin stepped into the tent. "A fairy is here to bring you to the castle."

Nimue looked at the soothsayer, then the new woman, and nodded. "Come, then. I have a lot to do and not much time to do it. We have a queen to coronate."

Red looked at me. "Then let us be away. I will call for you soon. I know your heart breaks to be away from your paramour, but just know that your continued absence keeps her safe."

"Thank you, my friend," I replied. "That doesn't help at all."

Red shrugged. "Well, I tried."

CHAPTER 36
RED

"You do understand that if you don't bring us straight to the throne room, I will rip you apart?" I muttered to the glowing white fairy as she hovered in front of the soothsayer's tent.

"Pfft," the fairy replied in a high, nasal voice. "You can try. Where's the other one? The Gorgon?"

"Don't worry about her," I snapped. "She's staying behind for the moment. She has unfinished business with the Mountain people." I wanted to slam the fairy straight into the Wall of Itherium for speaking to me in such an insolent manner, and rub its face across the grooved runes carved into every brick in the two-hundred foot wall that separated us from Hera's Dark Domain.

"That's not the order—"

"I don't care about the order," I snarled. "Take us back to the castle."

"Queen Aine will not be happy about this."

"Well, she can join the club," Nimue added from the end of her leash. "Do you think I wanted to be walked around like a rabid dog today?"

"Rabid dogs aren't walked," I replied. "They're shot."

Nimue sighed. "Well, the way this conversation's going, that might be an upgrade."

I pressed my fingers to my temples. "Just get us out of here, okay?"

"It shall be done," the fairy said. She snapped her fingers and we disappeared. When we reappeared and the light dissipated, I was on unstable footing, fighting to clutch Chelle's book in one hand and Nimue's leash in the other.

"Chelle!" I heard Rose cry out as her feet pattered across the throne room. When she saw that Chelle wasn't with us, she froze in place on the black carpet. "Chelle...isn't here. Where is she?"

I worked to regain my composure. "We should talk about that in private, ma'am."

Rose took a step back and spoke in a haughty tone. "Do not treat me like a child. I am the Queen of Oz. Tell me now."

I looked over at Queen Aine, floating near the makeshift altar being built over the throne. "I don't think this is something you want her knowing, ma'am."

"Oh, I already know," Queen Aine replied. "I thought you would be too dumb to realize it, but I know exactly why Chelle isn't with you."

"And why is that?" Rose said, spinning around to the fairy queen.

"Because they know that the minute Chelle shows back up, my pact with her is done, and they don't want to relinquish my power until at least the coronation. Isn't that so?"

I nodded. "That's right."

"She will have to come back to this castle eventually. She can't stay hidden forever."

"Ozma stayed hidden for a hundred years."

"Yes, but it was not forever, was it? And a hundred years is nothing when it comes to Urgu."

"This sucks!" Rose cried, throwing her hands in the air. "I want to see Chelle. You need to take me to her."

I shook my head. "Are you kidding? There's a coronation, Nimue to deal with, and this book that you're supposed to decode. There's no time. Chelle still has her pendant, and you can talk to her, okay? But right now, seeing her is just gonna have to wait."

Queen Aine nodded in agreement. "She's right. The coronation is upon us, and there is still so much to do." She gestured back to the altar behind her. "The altar is not even half built yet."

"Being queen blows," Rose replied.

"I know, but it is your burden."

"Just know," Queen Aine said. "that I will not be tricked into helping Rose one minute longer than the coronation. I have my own people to look after, and once she is queen, somebody else can take over."

I nodded. "That is amenable to me. I'm sure that Rose wants that as much as we do."

"I want Chelle to see my coronation, to see where all this is going. There has been so much pain—"

"I hate to break it to you, Rose," I replied, bowing my head. "I doubt that Chelle wants to see you as Queen. She's kind of hoping you'll forget about this all and come back home with her, seeing as she risked her life to get this book."

"I didn't ask her to do that!" Rose shouted.

"I know you didn't. You were very clear about that." I handed her the book. "But it's in your hands now. If you ask me, if you stay here, it's a slap in the face to me and everybody else here who would give everything to go back to Earth." I swallowed loudly. "Now, I must take care of Nimue. Where is Balor?"

"In the prison."

"He was supposed to stay with you."

"I know, but I had other needs of him. Besides, Queen Aine has done a fine job of protecting me."

I walked out of the throne room, tugging Nimue along. I looked at Rose one last time, looking down at the book. She was fighting back tears.

Nimue snickered. "Do you really think she could give all this up for love?"

"I don't know," I replied.

Nimue shook her head. "She has been touched by the gods. Not only does she have power, she *is* power. Back on Earth she will be nothing. Nobody can forego the power of the gods."

"Maybe not," I replied. "But I can still hope she will."

"And who will be the queen with her gone? You?"

"That's a problem for the future. Right now, I just hope she makes the right decision...as my friend."

"Pitiful," Nimue replied. "Absolutely pitiful. Don't you know that a queen can't have friends?"

I yanked her leash and she tripped forward. "Let's go."

ROSE

"I don't understand, Chelle," I said into the magic mirror projecting her face against the wall of my room. "I mean, I do understand, but I don't."

"We're trying to keep you safe," Chelle replied.

A tear fell down my cheek. "Why can Queen Aine keep me safer than you? You both have magic."

"Not the same magic, and not the same power. Plus, Queen Aine understands the life of the palace better than I ever could."

"Fine," I scowled. "Be that way. But you better be back for my coronation."

"I don't know if that's the best idea, I—"

"Listen!" I shouted. "I am about to be made queen. You are my girlfriend and you will be there, okay?"

"Is that...an order?" Chelle asked, confused.

I smiled through my tears. "You're damn right it is."

Chelle chuckled. "You know I think this is all stupid, right? Like, you should be coming home, with me."

I shook my head. "I know you think that, and I'm going to get you home, since you're so adamant about it, but if you want me to translate this stupid book, you better come back to the castle, okay? Otherwise, I'm going to burn it up and you'll never open that stupid Obsidian Spindle."

"Are you sure it's what you want? Being queen?"

I shook my head. "No, what I really want is to be with you, but I can't leave this place. I have a duty to Oz, to Urgu, and to Hypnos."

"Who cares?" Chelle replied. "Once Ozma died, Hypnos found you, and if you leave, then he'll find somebody else, or he won't, but we'll be back on Earth. Why do you care so much?"

Chelle would never understand. She would never see things like I saw them, but I couldn't stop from trying to make her see that Earth had nothing to offer me. "Because Earth sucks. If I go back with you, I'm going to have to figure out how to pay for my medications again, along with a hospital stay, with money I don't have. I mean, it's all bad, Chelle, it might as well be bad here, where I have magic."

Chelle sighed. "Fine, I'll come back for the coronation and you'll figure out the pages we need so that I can open the Spindle and go back to Earth."

"You'll go back to Earth without me."

"That's what I said."

My eyes narrowed. "I know what you said, and I know what you mean. You think I'll change my mind, but I won't."

"Yes, you are very stubborn, even when you're fighting against your own self-interest."

"So are you. Neither of us like to blink."

Chelle held her eyes wide and then blinked very over-dramatically. "Well, I'm blinking, Rose. If you want to stay in Urgu, you are an adult, I suppose that is your right."

"Thank you, Chelle. I'll let you know when I have the

spell."

"How long do you think?"

"I don't know. The coronation is tomorrow, and I've never translated a weird, old, golden book before, but I guess I'll be up all night figuring it out."

"Hey," Chelle said softly, "I love you."

There was a knock on the door, and Queen Aine stood in front of it. "I have to go."

The mirror turned off, and I turned toward her. "I'm very busy. Are preparations set for tomorrow?"

"They are, your majesty," Queen Aine said. "I am vexed about how your paramour has held me against my will to help you."

"I know," I replied. "Once I get this stupid spell translated, Chelle promised me she'll come back, and then you can go home."

"Thank you," she replied.

I stood up. "I hope you'll stay though, for the ceremony."

Queen Aine smiled. "It won't be by force."

"I know. I want you to stay because you are my friend."

Queen Aine turned away from me. "Humans don't make friends with fairies, especially Unseelie ones."

"This is a new day, and this queen does make friends with Unseelie queens."

Queen Aine's light flickered brighter for a moment. "That is very nice of you. As a queen, there are not many people I can turn to for friendship."

"I expect I will find much of the same."

"You will. There are not many alive who can speak to the trials of running a kingdom. You happen to have three of them in this castle."

"One of them will be dusted in the morning, if I have

any say in the matter, and, as queen, I do."

"Don't be so quick to kill Nimue, your majesty. She can still be helpful."

"How? As a totem for my conspirators?"

Queen Aine pointed to the golden book on my bed. "She studied more about how to get out of Urgu than anybody, and she has more experience dealing with the nobles than anyone else."

"I opened the book already," I said. "I could see the symbols inside, but I couldn't understand them. They were like reading a series of squiggly lines and M.C. Escher paintings."

"And that is how Nimue can be helpful. She's studied the ancient texts and could help you understand them."

"This is not a ploy to help your friend?"

Queen Aine shook her head. "Nimue and I were never friends, because I have never had a friend. Until now, at least."

I smiled. "I hope you're not lying to me. I am very gullible."

"I'm not."

I grabbed the book with both hands. "Very well, I'll go see Nimue, against the very fiber of my being."

"Go with the gods," Queen Aine replied. "I have more final details to prep. Only about a million of them. Why is everything so hectic until it comes together at the last moment?"

I chuckled as I walked out. "It's always the way."

I had promised Chelle to translate the spell that would open the Obsidian Spindle, and even if my stomach sank when I thought of her, Nimue was the greatest scholar of the Spindle I knew. I just hoped she could help me and do it without making me want to dust her.

CHAPTER 38

CHELLE

She'll understand. She might not like me at first, but she'll understand. I can't let her stay in the Dream Realm. I can't let her stay in Urgu. It's not safe.

"She won't understand," the soothsayer said in a knowing voice from across the tent from me. "She will forgive you because she loves you, but she will never understand."

"What do you know?" I scoffed.

"Much."

I turned to her. "Then tell me how this will all end."

"I can't. If I do, it will change the outcome."

"So?"

"It is already hanging on by a thread, if I were to tip it one way or the other, there would be dire consequences." A shriek pierced the windows and filled the air. "Ah, there they are. I wondered how long it would take for the shadow demons to arrive."

"The shadow demons! They're here?!"

"Of course. Did you think Hera would just give up?"

I would never give up. This was always my intention. It was inevitable.

"Get out of my head," I grumbled to her.

Make me.

I didn't have time to deal with Hera's bullshit. I rushed outside of the tent and looked up at the sky. Thousands of yellow eyes peeked through the dark over the Wall of Itherium. After a moment, the soothsayer came to join me, as the rest of the Mountain people rushed out of their tents with their weapons.

"I thought this wall was magic and protected the people of Oz," I said to the Soothsayer.

"It does," she replied. "That is why the Shadow demons are not through yet. However, Hera has powerful magic, too, and with the Emerald City's gaze on the coronation, this is the perfect time to attack."

My demons cannot attack the Land of Oz, unless something is stolen from me, and then, I am allowed to retrieve it. With brute force if necessary.

"Oh no," I said.

You walked into my trap.

"We have to do something," I said to the collected group around me.

"I can teach you a spell that will give us more time, but it will drain your aura considerably," the soothsayer said to me. "We are not strong enough to perform this alone, but with you, the Mountain People can direct a powerful light upwards that will dissipate the night, for a moment at least."

"And then what?"

"And then, you go back to the castle. Have Rose raise the defenses. They are coming for her, and for you."

"What defenses?"

"Ask Nimue. She will know."

"And what about you?" Another, even louder screech pierced through the air. The shadow demons seemed to mold from many bodies into one, and their mass shook the Wall, sending bits of it to the ground.

"My people have requested asylum in the Emerald City, and our petition has always been denied. They demanded me as prisoner, and though I offered myself as sacrifice, every member of the Mountain clan voted against it. I cannot—"

"You won't have to do that. Not today," I replied. "You'll come with me and we'll get you out. I'll get you all out, and you will be free. I swear it."

"That is what we've been waiting for."

This was the end game the soothsayer had always known about and had been preparing for. I had bigger problems, like saving the Land of Oz.

"What is the spell?"

"*Lux deum. Influunt per me,*" the soothsayer replied. "You must say it like you mean it. EVERYONE, gather around!"

I looked down into my locket. "Rose, Rose, Rose. We need your help. We need you to send a fairy now. Now, Rose!" But there was nobody at the other end of the line. The Queen's chambers were empty.

The shadow demons shrieked and rumbled over the wall. Two soldiers fell from the top, screaming all the way down until they dusted on the ground. Above, more shadow demons looked to strike.

I couldn't wait. I held my arms into the air. "*Lux deum! Influunt per me!*"

A bolt of light shot from my body. I looked around to see the light from the others mixing with mine. "It's working!"

"Don't stop!" the soothsayer called out.

My knees were weak. This spell took everything out of me, and the groans from around me told me it was taking it all from the Mountain People, too. With one final burst, I fell to my knees, and there was a ball of light, like a giant sun held in the air. The shadow demons scrambled backwards, scalded by the light.

The ball of light didn't last long, and as soon as I stopped concentrating, two purple eyes appeared, swallowing the light completely.

Good effort. Not enough, though. Soon, I will overtake the Land of Oz, and even Hypnos won't be able to stop me.

"Rose!" I shouted into the locket. "Please!"

But still there was nothing, and I knew then that with the wall breached, we were going to die. I was sick of feeling like I was going to die. I just wanted to go home, where the worst monsters I had to deal with were bounty hunters, who weren't that big a deal compared to vengeful gods and magic-hungry queens.

CHAPTER 39
NIMUE

I expected Rose to come. She was just a child-queen, after all, and I had ruled for over a hundred years. I expected her to walk down the dungeon stairs with her head slung low, carrying the golden book which I had spent so much time studying, even if every page was blank to me.

But she didn't walk like a nervous child anymore. Something had happened to her over the few days of her reign. Her gait was nearly regal, though she still slumped her shoulders. I could see that the confidence behind her eyes was little more than false bravado, but she put on a good enough show that others might be fooled.

"Leave us," Rose said, walking up to Red and the bushy-haired lout who guarded me.

Red looked up, startled. "But your majesty, what if—"

"Leave me," Rose repeated, more sternly than the first time. It was regal, the way she refused to accept sass back from her staff, though a real queen would not have gotten sass in the first place.

Red straightened her shoulders. "Yes, queen. Where should I—?"

"My quarters." Rose spoke in a loud, clear voice, enunciating each syllable. "Wait for Chelle to call until I return. If she does, come and find me."

"I'm not your errand girl," Red said.

Rose put her hand up to silence her. "That is exactly what you are, just as you have been for my predecessors. Now, please. Go. Leave me to my business."

Red's cheeks flushed and she glared at the floor, but she didn't say another word. She gestured to Balor, who stood up and walked out with her, scratching his head.

"That was downright cruel," I said to Rose when she slid down onto a stool next to me. "I loved it."

"I don't mean to be cruel," Rose said with a defeated sigh. "But I have the weight of the whole kingdom on my shoulders, people trying to kill me at every turn, and I can't have somebody questioning my authority."

I erupted in a fit of giggles. I couldn't contain how much Rose's words tickled me.

"What?" Rose said, cocking her head. "Stop laughing at me."

I swallowed my laughter. "I'm sorry. It's just...I never thought I would have something in common with you, is all."

Scorn fell over Rose's face. "We are nothing alike."

"Aren't we?" I leaned closer to her. "I wasn't always like this, you know. There was a time when I was wild eyed and naïve, just like you. Being queen hardens you. I dealt with ten assassination attempts before my coronation. How about you?"

"Three," Rose replied.

"Three?" I took a deep breath, before allowing a small smile to crest across my face. "Wow. Somebody must like you."

She bowed her head. "It doesn't feel like it."

I shook my head. "No, it never does, because you are no longer a human to them. You are a queen; an object. Your opinions only matter because you wear the crown. Once you no longer do, and your power fades, well," I gestured to the cell, "you end up like this."

"There has to be a different way. Hypnos wouldn't—"

"Please don't say that name," I grumbled. My back prickled at the invocation of the gods. "The gods don't care about us, darling. Look at me. I was a means to an end for Hera, and you are a means to an end for Hypnos, just as Ozma was before you."

Rose leaned into the iron bars, desperate for answers. I remembered when I was so naïve, and how nobody helped me. "What end?"

"I don't know, frankly," I replied after a long moment. There was no point in lying. Besides, the truth would bring her closer to me. If we bonded, perhaps I could sway her to my will. "I thought I knew once. I thought it was to get out of this place, but now—we were so close. If Hera truly wanted to leave Urgu, she would have never taken my powers from me. She would have let me continue my work. She would have let me attack..."

I didn't want to say the next words for fear it would provoke Rose, but she looked at me sweetly. She knew exactly what I was going to say but didn't seem to care. "It's okay. You can say it."

I pushed the word out against its will. "—you."

"Perhaps she was waiting until we had this." Rose tapped the golden book.

The golden book of Hypnos. How long I had wished to read the blank pages which only revealed themselves to the true queen of Urgu. "I thought that maybe when I became queen, its secrets would reveal themselves to me, but I was wrong."

"They did to me, but I can't read their words."

Of course they would reveal themselves to a whelp like Rose. She had everything, including my life. "Do you want to read it?" I asked. "If the only thing that could happen is to lead you home?"

"No," Rose replied. "Yes? I don't know. I'm so conflicted. I want to be queen, but...I hate the way it makes me feel. I hate all of this...and then I talk to Chelle, and she wants so badly to go home, and I fight her there as well, because it means giving all this up."

"Maybe you could find your way back here one day," I replied.

"Not as a queen."

"No, just as a dreamer, which has its own charms. You could explore the Sandlands, or the Bogs, or the Mistreach. Perhaps you could start a new life there, far from this place."

"Nobody has any idea how to bring dreamers back here," Rose said. "I doubt this book even says how."

I shook my head. "That book is nothing but a list of spells that make this place function. It's a user manual, at best. It's the first book Hypnos ever made and was supposed to be used by the queen should anything happen to him. Yet, when the moment came when this book could have been useful to Ozma, I drove her into exile, and kept the book for myself."

Rose looked up from the book and caught my eyes. "Do you think you can help me find the spell?"

I shook my head. "I can't read it."

"No, but you can translate it, right? If I copied down what I saw on ink and parchment?"

"Possibly," I nodded. "I found some original writings a queen made of some of the pages centuries ago. From them, I learned the language of the gods. They showed me how to lower the defenses to this castle and allow Hera to enter."

"Defenses?"

"Oh yes, hundreds of them, and the spell is in that book, and in my head."

"So can you help me?"

I nodded. "For a price."

The gods' price for reading their language was pain. Translating the words if you weren't the true queen brought me great misery and torture. My nose bled and my head throbbed. It felt as though my entire body would break apart with every word I learned, and I wasn't about to give them to a whelp child to use without having her give me something in return.

Rose sneered. "You have little to bargain with."

I smiled. "False. I have knowledge, which is the greatest bargaining power in the world."

Rage boiled in Rose's eyes. "What do you want?"

I gave her a coy look. Now we were bargaining. "I want to attend your coronation, my dear. I want to see how this all plays out."

Rose swallowed, trying desperately to maintain her composure, but failing. "You want to be there if they kill me, to take my crown."

I shrugged. "That would be a nice side effect, but mostly, I just love a spectacle."

"And what do I get out of this?"

"I will give you the spell to raise the defenses on this castle and tell you the exact page I need translated from the book to open the Obsidian Spindle. That way, you have a choice. You can either keep the kingdom or escape from it."

"I...don't...know..."

I smiled. The child was in over her head, but flattery was everything when dealing with a monarch, so it was important to swallow my pride and hide my intentions behind pleasant lies. "You are a deft negotiator. Very well. I will do you one better. I will give you the spell to see the soul of your conspirators and know which of your subjects is a traitor to the crown. Then, you will know who tried to kill you, and deal with them in whatever way you see fit."

Rose's eyebrows shot up. "You can do that?"

I nodded. "Magic can do everything, my dear. Has Queen Aine taught you nothing?"

"Well, we've been very busy."

Perhaps I could sow doubt between her and her consort. "I'm sure you have, chasing your tails. That is very like her."

"What does that mean?"

"Nothing," I replied. "Do we have a deal?"

"It's not a very good deal if I decide to leave."

I smiled. "No, only if you decide to stay, but we both know that you will. You are so very like me in that manner."

"What manner is that?" Rose asked.

"When you attain true power, you are unable to give it up, like a drug. You could never leave this place, and become a—what is it—a nothing burger again, could you?" Of course, I would give it up, give it all up, to return to a body, but Rose didn't know that, and I dared not tell her. "Doesn't the power feel good, flowing through your veins?"

"Maybe..."

"Have you ever felt anything like it?"

She shook her head. "No."

"Don't you feel invincible right now?"

"I do," she said, nodding emphatically.

"Like nothing would dare touch you; like nothing could touch you?"

She grabbed onto the bars of the cell. "Yes, yes I do."

"And you really believe you could give all that up, willingly?" I scoffed. "Please. That is just a lie you are telling yourself. Take the deal. It's the best you'll get from me."

Rose thought for a moment, but I knew she couldn't turn down my proposal. "Very well, if you give me the spell to raise the castle defenses and to see my enemies, then I will let you come to the ceremony."

Poor child. She had lost and didn't even know it yet. "Oh no. I'm afraid it doesn't work like that. I will give you the spell to raise the defenses now, and then, the moment you are queen, I will give you the second spell to find the traitors, and you will give me the page from the golden book, which I will translate for you."

"And then you will die," Rose said.

We'll see about that. "That's not very kind."

"You weren't very kind."

I grinned broadly. "Let me at least stay for cake."

"Very well," she said with a definitive nod. "After cake, you will be dusted in the square as my first official act as queen, along with all who oppose me."

Rose stood up to leave the dungeon after making her pronouncement. I stood as well and bowed. "You are harsh, but fair. May the Red Queen reign for a thousand years."

I should have feared for my life, but I was rejoicing inwardly. I had managed to buy myself forty-eight more hours of life. In that moment, I felt like I could do anything.

CHAPTER 40
RED

"Can you believe this, Balor?" I said as we walked toward Rose's room. "She's treating us like we're slaves, or something.

"Aye, or like we're here to do what she says," Balor said, then paused. "Say, aren't we here to do what she says, though?"

"I suppose. But she doesn't have to be so mean about it."

"ROSE! ROSE!" I heard from inside the room. It was Chelle's voice. I pushed open the door and saw the Gorgon's face plastered on Rose's mirror.

"Chelle!" I ran to the mirror. "What's going on?"

I couldn't see much except her face surrounded by darkness. All around her, people were screaming, and the shrieks of shadow demons filled the air.

"Red!" Chelle screamed. "You're a sight for sore eyes. We're being attacked by shadow demons."

"That's impossible. The Wall of—"

"I don't care what the wall's supposed to do!" Chelle

said. "It's not doing it. We have to get out of here right now."

"We?"

"Me, all the soldiers, and all the refugees. We're getting slaughtered out here."

"There's a tree, in the woods—"

"We don't have time for that!" Chelle shouted. "We need fairies, and we need them now!"

"Okay!" I replied. "Hang tight!"

The mirror went dark. Balor followed me out of the room and down the hallway toward the kitchen. I had to find Queen Aine. I had heard her in there, shouting at the bakers while we were on our way to Rose's room.

"And this is not how you lay fondant, Charles. Who taught you baking?" Queen Aine yelled at a frightened half-orc chef.

"Sorry, ma'am," the chef whimpered. "It's usually the head chef who does this, but he's disappeared."

"No excuses," Queen Aine snapped. "Get it done and do it right."

"Queen Aine," I said, rushing through the door. "We need your help. The Gates of Droangor are under attack."

She didn't take her eyes off of the chef cowering by the table. "So?"

"People are dying, including Chelle."

"Good," Queen Aine said. "Traitorous bitch, if you ask me."

"Sure, but if she doesn't come back, you'll never get out of your deal with her. If you save her—"

"Then I'll end my deal with her immediately!" Queen Aine looked at me and smiled. "Stay here." She vanished, and a moment later she reappeared with four shining white guards. "Let's go."

Balor and I unsheathed our weapons, ready to fight. Queen Aine snapped her fingers, and with a crackle and flash we were back in the refugee camp. A huge ball of light surrounded us, and thousands of little yellow eyes flew everywhere, slamming against it with all their might.

"*Lux*!" Chelle shouted. She was right in front of me. "*LUX*!"

"Chelle!" I screamed.

Chelle held up her arms, struggling against the weight of the shadow demons bearing down on her shield, and looked at me. "Oh, thank the gods you're here."

"Is this everyone? We have to go now."

"*Lux*!" Chelle shouted and a shadow demon shriveled at my feet.

"Enough!" Queen Aine shouted. The light from her body grew until it covered the camp, sending the shadow demons flying backward. "Get close to me! All of you!"

The refugees and soldiers fled into her protective light as the shadow demons screamed and sizzled at its touch. Balor and I stood on the edge of the light with Chelle, ready to attack in case anything came inside.

When the last of the soldiers were within the light, Queen Aine nodded to her troops and we vanished into the night, nearly overrun by the shadows.

CHAPTER 41

ROSE

Stomping down the hallway after my visit with Nimue, I heard a commotion in the throne room and rushed toward it. The carpenters had been working all night to erect the stage, and I thought they had made a mistake, and something collapsed. When I entered the throne room, however, I found not the carpenters, but a dozen soldiers, a half-dozen fairies, and so many people with neon hair, eyes, and black clothes that I thought I was at a rave.

"*Lux!*" Chelle shouted.

Tears sprang into my eyes when I saw her, and I wanted to rush to her, but she was in trouble. Several black smoke demons with bright eyes and long arms were entangled with Chelle and the others. I couldn't help without the possibility of hurting the innocent, but I could save them if I rebooted the castle's defenses. I ran to the balcony just like Nimue had told me and found the innocuous statue of an old woman looking out over the city.

Remembering Nimue's instructions, I dropped the golden book and placed my hands on the statue's face.

"Spirit of Nox, protect this palace from all magical creatures that wish to disturb it."

The eyes of the old woman opened, and a light blue shimmer filled them, then washed down her arms and body, onto the balcony. The old woman transformed into a beautiful young nymph with long wings and a bright smile as the blue light cascaded through the castle and rippled over the roof.

The black demons hissed and moaned before dissolving, and once the blue wash had run its course, a loud, deep echo reverberated throughout the castle.

"What happened?" Queen Aine asked.

"I used the spell that Nimue taught me which banished all magical creatures that would do us harm." I smiled at her. "And yet, you are still here."

"Yes, I am, aren't I?" Queen Aine smiled. "Which means I've been telling the truth this whole time. Maybe now you'll believe me."

I nodded. "It's not that I didn't believe you before, but it's nice to have confirmation. I've had to deal with so many people lying to me, recently."

I turned my attention to the group of people who had appeared in my throne room. Chelle emerged from the crowd, now free of her tormentor. and I couldn't help the smile cracking on my face when she came running toward me.

"Babe!" Chelle shouted at me before wrapping her arms around me and giving me a long kiss. "I missed you so much. So much. You don't even know."

I smiled and kissed her again. "I do a little. I missed you, too."

Chelle wrapped her arms around me. "The last couple of days have been bananas."

I looked over at Queen Aine, then back to Chelle. I had a coronation the next day, and I had to draw a page from the golden book before then, but these things were all secondary to seeing Chelle again.

My smile broadened and tears rolled down my face. "I can't wait to hear about it." Her snakes cooed at me and I pet each of them in turn. "You missed me too, huh?"

"We all missed you," Chelle said. She was staring into my face when her smile dissolved. "Rose...where is the book? Tell me you have the book!"

"Oh! I left it on the patio." I wiped my face with the sleeve of my dress, overwhelmed with emotion and all the things that needed doing. "I need to look through it to translate it tonight."

"I'll grab it for you." Chelle replied. She headed towards the patio then stopped and looked over her shoulder at me. "So, you're coming back with me, then?"

My eyes dropped to the floor. "We can talk about it later. I'm sure you're tired, and I have a big day tomorrow. Let's go to bed."

Queen Aine fluttered up to me when Chelle had walked away.

"You can go now, if you want," I said.

Queen Aine wagged her finger. "I have something more to do, yet, and that is to make you a queen. I'll go once the coronation ceremony finishes. Besides, what would people think if the queen of fairies left before you were crowned?"

"Not...nice...things?"

"Not nice at all."

Queen Aine floated away toward her bed chamber and was replaced by Red, alongside a tall woman with red eyes and red dreads mixed in with her black hair.

"Your majesty, this is Boudica, queen of the Mountain people."

I dipped my head toward her. "How do you do?"

"Poorly, your majesty. My people have been through great hardship. We've petitioned you for a long time, but with deaf ears as a response."

"These people are all your charges?"

Boudica looked back at them. "Aye, all that's left. I don't have much to offer you. We have some magic but it's not like yours. It's...ours."

Boudica turned and the Mountain people parted. In the middle of them were two women. Their faces were covered in plaster and glass. Behind their masks, dust billowed, and clouds formed in a torrent of dark energy.

"This is the soothsayer," Red said. "She has cheated death like few others in all Urgu, even the gods. If you let us stay here, she will teach you all she knows."

I walked forward. I realized that her face was not a mask, but a vessel for her doomed soul thrashing behind the glass. "Is this your dusted soul you have kept here?"

"Very good, your majesty," the soothsayer replied, without moving her porcelain mouth.

My eyes went wide. "Fascinating."

"Do we have a deal?" Boudica said.

"No," I replied. The group gasped. "You may stay because you are in trouble, and I extend my hand to you in friendship." I placed my hands softly on the porcelain black hands of the soothsayer. "If you choose to impart your wisdom to me otherwise, then we will discuss it later, after the coronation." I looked back to see Chelle, who was walking towards me clutching the book. "Now, if you'll excuse me, I must be going. Red, Balor, if you can make sure our guests are comfortable, I would appreciate it."

"Of course, ma'am."

"And...Red?"

"Yes, ma'am."

"I'm sorry."

"Thank you, ma'am."

I placed my hand on the small of Chelle's back, and together we walked out of the throne room, toward my bed chamber. The thought of laying my head on her chest and listening to her sleep, just that tiny act, was thrilling to me.

Tomorrow, there would be arguments, and fracturing, but now, for this moment, we could just be happy, and leave that heartbreak for our future selves to deal with.

CHAPTER 42

CHELLE

I woke up from a fitful sleep to see Rose sitting at her desk, lit only by candlelight. She looked down at the golden book, and then, with a quill pen, transcribed something onto a piece of parchment.

"What are you doing?" I asked, rubbing my eyes.

Rose jumped. "Oh, I'm sorry. Did I wake you?"

"Of course not, you're quiet as a mouse."

I pushed myself off the bed and walked over to her. The golden book was completely blank to me, but Rose saw something on its pages. Her eyebrows furrowed as she stared at it, and then copied shapes onto a piece of parchment.

"Is this it?" I asked.

Rose nodded. "According to Nimue, it is the page which will open the Spindle and bring you home."

The words Rose wrote looked like nothing I had ever seen before. They were loops that went on for three lines that looked identical in every way, like a cursive S repeated a hundred times, and then large circles that floated around the page. It looked more like an abstract art painting than words.

I kissed Rose on the shoulder. "Are you sure this is wise? Trusting Nimue."

"No," she said. "But this is the only option we have right now. Trust her and hope she doesn't betray us or stay in the Dream Realm together. Personally, I would rather not do this at all and have you stay here with me."

"I want us to be together, but on Earth," I replied.

Rose snorted loudly. "Yes, you have made your feelings well known. I just wish you would consider mine as well."

"And what are your feelings, Rose? You seem to hate this place and love it at the same time."

"That's exactly it. I've never felt so alive, Chelle, but I've also never felt so alone. You make me feel like I can do anything, and here I can."

"What about Earth?"

"Every time I think about Earth, all I remember is us struggling to survive. I think about me needing my medicine and fighting to live every single day. Look at this. This is paradise. We have everything we could ever need."

"Except bodies. Except lives. Except anything we remember. Look around, you're writing with a feather! This is absurd. There are cars on Earth. There's air conditioning. There's TV. That magic mirror is literally not even a big deal on Earth, because we have Facetime. You're the most powerful person on this planet, and we can't even watch *The Simpsons*."

"We could make *The Simpsons*," Rose said, turning to me.

"We don't have to make it. We can go back to Earth and watch it."

"I mean, eww, why would we do that, though?"

"We don't have to watch that show. We can watch something better. There are literally thousands of shows and millions of books, and, oh yeah, there's also magic on Earth."

"Not for me."

"So what?"

"So, I like being powerful. I like feeling powerful. I like that these people look to me."

"That they're trying to kill you?"

"Yeah, a little bit. Better than being completely ignored."

"No, it's not. And I never ignored you."

"You were the only one."

I swallowed and then dropped my head. "Aren't I enough?"

There was a long pause before Rose finally said, "I have to finish this before they come to get me into my dress."

"So that's it then. It's your own magic over me."

Rose sat back down. "It doesn't have to be, but we've both made up our minds, and we're both pretty stubborn."

"That we are."

Rose looked at me. "This might be the last day we spend together, Chelle. Let's just try to make it a happy one, so we can have one last happy memory, before the end."

"I don't know if I can do that."

"I'm not saying you can. I'm just saying to try. Please, for me."

"Fine," I replied, and I sat down on the couch next to her and listened to her write until I fell asleep again, hoping to dream of a simpler time.

CHAPTER 43

ROSE

Chelle didn't have the luxury of staying up all night, since she still had her body and thus needed to rest. I could, though, since I was nothing but a soul in Urgu. By morning, I had finished transcribing the page. I would have been done sooner, but every time I messed up on one character or another, I had to start over. Nimue told me it had to be perfect.

"Are you ready, my dear?" Queen Aine said, walking through the door with two young girls and a long white dress.

"Am I to be married?" I asked, standing from my desk.

"In a way," Queen Aine said. "You are marrying Urgu, but more importantly, when Nimue was coronated, she wore black, so I thought that the opposite would be nice for you to show this is the birth of a new day."

I nodded. "That sounds good. I told you to figure it out, and so I'm just going to pretend all of this is perfect no matter what I think about anything."

"You don't have to do this," Chelle said, wiping the sleep from her eyes.

"I want to do it. If you don't like it, you can wait outside. A girl only gets coronated once in their lives."

"That's right," Queen Aine said, wagging her finger. "And we won't have any negativity."

"Fine," Chelle replied. "I won't say anything, since I have nothing nice to say."

"Acceptable," I smiled at her as Queen Aine and her assistants set out the things they'd need to get me ready.

I had never seen something so beautiful and elegant in my life as the dress Queen Aine chose for me, and when I stepped into it, I felt every bit the queen. The corset was tight and dug into my ribs, but the cascading effect of my dress down my shoulders, around my waist, and then out for ten feet behind me was worth it.

They made me up to look every bit the white queen to counteract Nimue's black one, a symbol of rebirth and light for a world that had known too much sorrow and pain for the last century. They wrapped my hair up in metal rollers so that they bounced in large curls around my head, then they placed white oleanders and beads through it to match the flower accents on my cape.

When I was done, I looked over at Chelle. "How do I look?"

"Beautiful," Chelle said, weeping. "As beautiful as I always knew you would look at our wedding."

Her crying made tears well in my own eyes. "No, don't you do that. I can't go through the makeup process again. These girls will kill me."

One of the girls gasped. "We would never, lady."

"Oh, I know," I said dismissively. "It's just a thing that we say."

"Please don't say that, ma'am," the other one piped in. "We could be found guilty of treason and dusted."

Queen Aine floated up to me. "You must be careful with every word now, as they all have meaning, and will be taken seriously."

"Every word?" I said.

Queen Aine nodded. "Every. Word."

"That doesn't sound fun."

"The job of a queen isn't to have fun. It is to lead."

"That sounds like even less fun."

"You can still punt this," Chelle murmured. When I gave her a stern look, she threw up her hands. "I'm just saying."

After that, I was led down the hallway to await the entrance of the Cardinal of the Six, who would ordain me. The ceremony was to be held in the throne room, but I wouldn't enter until it was time to pronounce me queen. Being alone in the hallway with nobody but Queen Aine for comfort made me nervous.

"What if they try to attack me?" I said.

"I have that covered," Queen Aine replied.

I looked up at the paintings of writhing monsters. My first act as queen would be to replace them with something brighter and more festive, like the flowers that festooned the entrance to the castle.

"How?" I asked.

"Those nice Mountain People agreed to provide additional protection around the castle today."

"How do we know we can trust them?"

"Well, they weren't under Nimue's payroll, plus they arrested her and brought her to the Gates of Droangor, and you gave them protection when Nimue would not, so I would surely choose them over your other guards."

"And how do I know I can trust you?"

Queen Aine's smile faded. "Because we are friends, and friends trust each other."

Before I could reply, a hunchbacked old woman covered with wrinkles hobbled up to me. She carried a small book in one hand and in the other, a large cane ornamented with a blue tiger at the top of it. She leaned against the cane for support.

On either side of her walked one of the Mountain People, clad in the black garb of their kind and wearing the same neon that they did the previous night. They were a sight to behold.

"Queen Rose," Queen Aine said. "This is Her High Majesty Pious Edwina Lumpkin Jabberwocky."

I curtsied as much as possible in my constricting frock. "Nice to meet you."

"Edwina has been around as long as the Six."

"Longer!" Edwina replied. "I was here when it was only three. What a turbulent time it was."

"A pleasure to make your acquaintance."

"Yes, yes. You should know that I have presided over every coronation for the past three thousand years, and I will make sure this one goes off without a hitch."

I smiled. "Oh, you have never seen one like this."

Edwina leaned in and eyed me closely. "I have seen everything."

She sounded offended at my little joke, so I bit my tongue, remembering the solemnity of this day. "Of course, your piousness."

"This will be a short affair, if you don't mind. I will say a prayer to the Heavens, announce you. Then, you come forward. I will crown you, then you will officially be queen. After that, we'll have a nice supper. Won't that be nice?"

I nodded. "That does sound nice."

"Not for you, of course, as you will be whisked away to change, and then have to deal with all of the nobles in the

Emerald City, who all have things to discuss with you. But it will be nice for me.”

“Wonderful.”

“Again, not for you.”

“Hey, Rose?” Chelle was standing behind me. She looked sheepish. “Can we talk?”

I turned back to Edwina. “Go ahead,” the old woman said. “I have things to prepare. I still get a bit of stage fright, even after all these years.”

Queen Aine floated next to Edwina as they walked toward the throne room. I could hear the murmuring of the guests from where I was standing.

“What do you want?” I asked Chelle. “I’m not going to have another argument with you. Not now.”

“I don’t want to have an argument. This might be the last day we spend together. I just wanted to say that I love and support you.”

“You have a funny way of showing it.”

“I know, but I do. I really want what’s best for you. Sometimes I think I know what you want better than you do, but I know that’s not fair. If this is what you want, then you should have it, all of it.”

I smiled. “Thank you. What I really want is for us to be together, and happy, here.”

Chelle shook her head. “I can’t be happy here. I still have a body. Maybe, one day we’ll figure out how to let dreamers back in here, and then I can visit. Of course, you’ll likely have moved on by then.”

“Never,” I said in a huff.

“It’s okay. We’re both making a choice.” She touched my hands softly. “I love you. I’ll always love you. You know that, right?”

“I love you, too.”

Chelle pulled out a piece of parchment from her pocket. "You forgot this in the room."

I looked down. It was the piece of parchment I promised Nimue. I folded it in half and patted myself for a pocket, but found none, so I palmed it in my hand.

"That really sucks."

"It totally sucks."

Chelle reached toward me and gave me a soft kiss on the lips. I closed my eyes and savored the moment, knowing it would be one of the last we would share together, maybe ever.

The trumpets blared for me, and I knew it was time. "I have to go."

"I know."

I held the paper out in front of me. "Can you please sit next to Nimue on stage and hand this to her? The moment I'm crowned without incident, give it to her, and she will give you a spell to find my usurpers. Don't wait. Use it immediately. We can't afford to waste one second."

"I will, and I'll see you after."

I didn't know if that was true, but I still smiled and said, "Of course."

After the service, Chelle would give Nimue the page to translate, and then the Obsidian Spindle would be open, and Chelle would be gone. I regretted giving the paper to Chelle. I wanted to steal it back from her and burn it, but I wouldn't. I had made a promise, and just like Chelle wanted for me, I wanted her to be happy.

CHAPTER 44

RED

There must be an assassin in this audience somewhere. They'd already attempted to kill Rose multiple times before the coronation; certainly, they would try again during the ceremony, when she would be wide out in the open.

The throne room was packed to the gills with the influential men and women of Oz. The men of the small council sat in the front, the same men who had once pledged allegiance to Ozma, and then Nimue, and now to Rose. Next to them sat the soothsayer and Shaina, shrouded in cloaks so as to hide their porcelain bodies and not upset the others. The cardinals from the Church of the Six sat on the other side. Each of them presided over a different land of Urgu, and some of them had traveled thousands of miles to attend the event.

The rest of the room was filled with dignitaries, nobles, and the leisure class of Urgu. Outside, below the balcony, thousands gathered to pay witness to the queen when she greeted them from the balcony after her coronation. They chanted Rose's name from the palace square, where only weeks before Ozma had plummeted to her death.

"Should we close these?" I asked one of the Mountain People standing guard in front of the open windows.

"Queen Aine thinks that hearing the people chant Rose's name will convince the nobles not to kill her," Balor answered. He was standing behind me. "I think it's daft and foolish, but I'm only the help."

"Yeah," I said. "What do we know? We've only been protecting queens for hundreds of years."

"You should sit," Balor said, walking up to me as we passed in the center aisle of the throne room. "They are just about to sound the horn."

"I'll sit when she's coronated, and not before. Once she's queen, then we can protect her without a thousand duplicitous nobles hanging around her. We can find loyal men for her detail, and this will all be over."

"It's never going to be over, Belle. You know that."

I sighed. "Aye, I do, but a girl can dream, right?"

I pulled back the hood on my red cloak as the trumpets rang out in the throne room. Rose would be coming down the hallway any moment. I heard the jingling of chains, and watched Nimue walk into the room, escorted by a half dozen guards. They walked her up onto the altar constructed for the event and sat her in an open chair, next to Chelle, who was dressed in a tasteful black suit. Her snakes swung wildly around her head, and she reached up to calm them down, petting each in turn until they settled onto her head in a coil.

The side door to the throne room opened, and a small woman with a hunchback, wearing a dark red robe and a multicolored sash, hobbled up to the altar with the help of her cane. She was the highest of all the cardinals, Her High Majesty Pious Edwina Lumpkin Jabberwocky. The congregation stood solemnly to greet her.

She stood at the golden pulpit bejeweled with the sigils of the six; the peacock of Hera, the lioness of Sekhmet, the bloody sword of Agrona, the poplar tree of Hypnos, the spider of Anansi, and the snake of Loki.

"Let us pray!" Edwina said. "For the honor of the Six, let us bathe in their eternal glow, and keep holy their most sacred gift. Amen."

"Amen," the congregation murmured in one voice.

I looked over at Balor, and then up at Chelle, as the trumpets blared again and Rose entered the room, her head held high like a queen, shimmering in white like a goddess. My stomach sank because I didn't know what would happen next. All I could do was pray that her doom didn't come on this day.

CHAPTER 45
CHELLE

My jaw dropped when Rose walked into the room. She was glowing, radiant in a way I had never seen her. I'd seen her after the team of professionals made her up and dressed her, but there was something more, something inside of her. She was made for this moment. She had spent her whole life being a second fiddle, a shrinking violet to everybody else, and now she was the center of attention. All eyes were on her. She stopped and waved to the crowd, who stood and applauded her.

I seized the moment of distraction to turn to Nimue, as we both stood together to clap. I leaned over and whispered in her ear. "The minute she's crowned, I hand you the piece of paper, you will tell us the spell to denounce the traitors among us."

"I am on pins and needles," Nimue replied dryly.

After several minutes, the clapping died down. Edwina smiled at Rose, who was approaching the altar. As she passed the open window leading toward the balcony, I heard a whoosh and saw something whizzing through the air.

"Rose!" Red shouted from the audience, but I was ready.

"*Scutum caeli!*" I pushed my hands out in front of me and an air shield formed around the altar. There was a collective gasp as the arrow bounced off of the shield and fell to the ground. A black-clad figure jumped off the balcony onto the roof of the next building over. Red and Balor chased after him, and the crowd erupted in murmurs and exclamations.

After a moment I clapped my hands together. "Sorry, everybody. Please, continue."

The crowd calmed down. Rose smiled at me. She didn't seem fazed at all. "Thank you. How do I look?" She didn't have a single hair out of place.

"Majestic," I said.

I wasn't convinced that would be the only attack, but that was the most likely one, and at the most likely moment, too. Perhaps it was to get our guards up, and then down, or disrupt the ceremony, but after the arrow all of the windows and every door was closed. If there was another assassin, we were locked in with them now. Maybe that was the point.

"That was an adventure," Edwina said. "Perhaps we should continue, though, as there is still a queen to coronate today."

"Please," Rose said.

I sat down, and Edwina hobbled back to the pulpit. "Our new queen is a new arrival to Urgu, but she has seen much in her time here. I look forward to her gentle constitution guiding all the Dream Realm, now, and for the next hundred years. I am very old, and have been doing this a very long time, and I have lost my ability to pontificate for long stretches, so I will just get on with it. May I please have the box?"

One of the Mountain People scurried through the hallway carrying a red marble box. He struggled with its weight, and looked very out of place among the nobles, but I certainly trusted them more than the noblemen. With the doors closed, it was hard to make out anything except the purple and green highlights to his dreadlocked hair, which accented the goatee across his face.

"Here you go, ma'am."

The man opened the box and pushed it toward Edwina, who mumbled something under her breath and pulled out a white gold tiara adorned with diamonds, with six large gemstones circling its base: opal, obsidian, sapphire, ruby, emerald, and topaz.

"Queen Rose, this crown symbolizes your connection to the Six. These six gems represent each of the gods that you are sworn to protect." Bingo. "And the land you are meant to uphold. Do you swear to do your best to make the right decisions for Urgu, to put its needs even above your own, and live out your life in service to the Six?"

"I do," Rose replied.

"Then kneel."

Rose knelt and lowered her head. Edwina placed her hands on either side of the crown and placed it on Rose's head. "And rise, Queen Rose the First, dreamer turned regent of the Land of Oz!"

The crowd erupted in applause, and I caught Rose's eyes. She nodded to me. I took the piece of paper out of my suit jacket and handed Nimue the piece of parchment.

"What is the spell?" I said.

Nimue unfolded the paper. "How can I be sure this is a true transcription?"

"We'll just have to distrust each other."

Nimue chuckled. "Fair enough. The spell is *malignitatis excogitat, ostende te.*"

"Will that page really open the Obsidian Spindle?" I asked.

"We will soon find out."

Rose stood and greeted her public, and I stood with her. "*Malignitatis excogitat, ostende te.*"

For a moment nothing happened, and I was sure that Nimue had tricked us, but then, a small orange glow emanated from the crowd.

"Arrest that person!"

The Mountain People leapt into action to arrest a glowing man with a nose four times as big as his face. Then, another glow, and another, and another, and another. Soon, the entire congregation was glowing orange, all except for Nimue and Queen Aine, and the Mountain People. Even the cardinals glowed a dark orange.

"Oh no," I said. "Rose."

But it was too late. When I turned to the pulpit, Edwina had already pulled a dagger out of her robe and stabbed Rose in the back with it.

Rose let out a pained scream.

"*Fulminis!*" Lightning shot out of my hands and electrocuted Edwina before she could strike again. The crowd erupted in shrieks as they rushed from their chairs, but I didn't care about any of them. I rushed to Rose and scooped up her dying body. She was breaking apart in my hands.

"No, no, no, no, no!" I wailed. "Rose!"

I couldn't save my love. I had failed her.

CHAPTER 46
ROSE

Cold.

So cold.

Why am I so, so, cold?

I—I—I—am sorry.

CHAPTER 47

NIMUE

While the rest of the coronation was caught up in the excitement of Queen Rose's assassination attempt, I slipped off the dais and out the door in the back of the throne room. The guards, stationed at the entrance to the multicolored bridge which led to the Obsidian Spindle, had rushed to the queen's side, and so it was a simple matter to push open the door and walk out onto the bridge.

I looked down at the paper in my hands. A hundred years had come down to this moment, and I didn't even have to plunge the dagger into that worthless twerp's back myself. I unfurled the paper and studied it. I hadn't read the words of the old gods in at least thirty years and it took a few moments to come back to me. My brain hurt and my nose bled from the power contained in their writing, but it wasn't long before I decoded the spell.

"To force the Obsidian Spindle to open, place your hand on the door and speak these words true. I order you to open in the name of the old gods, the new, and the queen of Oz, the one true ruler of Urgu, and the defender of the realm from all who seek to destroy it. Hear my call, and open for me now."

Seemed easy enough. I knew there was an incantation to force open the door but did not know the words. I must have tried a thousand combinations, some even close to these, but none had worked. Now that I knew the words, they seemed trite and easy to guess, and yet, nobody ever had before.

I rolled up the scroll and stuffed it in my belt. I was still chained, but the restraints gave me enough freedom to walk briskly. Hopefully, briskly enough to escape the hydra in case it didn't remember me.

Then again, I'm not sure anything could be fast enough to avoid the attack of a seven-headed hydra. We had bonded, I hoped, over the many decades I was queen. I made a point of it. I anticipated she would be able to smell my scent and remember me.

If not, I had no recourse except death.

A shriek filled the air, and the bridge rumbled as the shadow of the hydra covered me in darkness. The sight of the sprawling menace filled me with dread. Even at full strength, I doubted I could take on the hydra, but I might stand a chance. Now, I would be defenseless if it chose to attack.

"Easy girl," I said calmly and gently, forcing a smile. "Do you remember me? I used to feed you steak. Remember?"

The beast snarled at me and one of its heads bent down low to investigate me, followed by another, and another, until all seven were within inches of my body, sniffing me. Their breath was hot and rotten on every inch of my body, and it was everything in my power not to shiver at the thought of a vicious death, but I held my composure, as a queen must do in every situation, and I was a rightful queen.

"Good girl," I said, holding out my hand toward one of its scaly heads.

It flinched for a moment, but then pushed back against my hand affectionately. My heartbeat fell back to normal, and I took a deep breath as the hydra pulled up and stomped back toward the gate entrance to the Spindle.

I stepped forward carefully, knowing that every movement meant the beast could change its mind, until I was facing the door to the Obsidian Spindle. I had been in this position a thousand times before, but never managed to open it.

"Here goes nothing," I said, placing my hand on the door. "I order you to open in the name of the old gods, the new, and the queen of Oz, the one true ruler of Urgu, and the defender of the realm from all who seek to destroy it. Hear my call, and open for me now."

A shockwave rippled through the door and cascaded across the bridge, throwing both me and the hydra backward. The door was silent for a moment, and then, the hinges shook, and the black door swung open for me, a great gust of air shooting out of it that smelled of musty, dank clothing soured in a storm.

I had done it. I had opened the Spindle, and I would be the first person in a hundred years to enter. I took a cautious step inside and the darkness engulfed me.

CHAPTER 48
RED

"Let me in!" I screamed, banging on the door to the castle's balcony. The attempted assassin got away before I got a good look at them, which meant I was in the dark as much now as I was before the attack, and Rose was still in danger.

"Let me in!" I shouted again. The door opened and I tumbled inside. "Finally! What are you—"

The entire throne room was pandemonium: Nobles lined up along the walls, people screaming, everybody glowing orange. "What is happening here?" And then I saw the altar. Rose was laying down, and I could see her breaking apart as Chelle held her in her arms.

"Rose!"

I rushed toward them. A guard tried to stop me, but I leapt across chairs to evade them, then I rolled onto the stage next to Chelle, still cradling Rose.

"What happened?"

"That bitch stabbed her." She pointed to a pile of ashy remains surrounding an old cane. Edwina. "She finished the ceremony, and then she stabbed her in the back. Help me."

Rose's eyes were closed, and she was turning pasty. Her hands were breaking into ash. I didn't know what I could do. It was only Queen Aine, who muttered a spell under her breath, that kept Rose from breaking apart completely.

"I'm sorry," Queen Aine said. "I can't hold her together for much longer."

"You'll hold her together for as long as I say!" Chelle screamed.

"You are not the queen!" Queen Aine shouted. "I take no orders from you."

"Please stop," I muttered. "There must be something we can do."

"There is no spell that can turn back death," Queen Aine said.

"She's not dead!" Chelle said. "She's not. She's not."

I had no idea what to do. I left Rose for five minutes, just five minutes, and she died. She was dead. *How could that be?*

"Excuse me?" I heard a voice behind me. "I can help." I turned to see the soothsayer and Shaina standing at the edge of the stage.

"How?" Chelle asked.

"She's...magic," I said. "She can save Rose's soul."

The soothsayer gently corrected me. "I am merely a vessel for an old spell that can bind the queen to this world."

"Bind?" Chelle said through her tears.

"She will become like me, and like my daughter," the soothsayer pointed to Shaina, who gave a slight nod. "But she will survive."

"No," Chelle said. "No way."

I put my hand on Chelle's shoulder. "It's the only option we have." I said, then looked at the soothsayer. "What do you need?"

"For the moment. I need a vessel, a porcelain pot, or something of clay that I can use for the binding."

"Right." I hopped to my feet. On either side of the altar were vases filled with long stemmed roses. I pulled out the flowers from one of them and dumped the water, then rushed it over to the soothsayer. "Will this work?"

She rubbed it slowly with her outstretched porcelain arm. "Yes, the pores are large enough to contain a soul. This will do. Please place it next to the queen."

I did so as the Soothsayer shuffled onto the stage with Shaina. They knelt on either side of Rose's body.

"I know this is hard," the Soothsayer said to Chelle. "But if you want to save your beloved, then you must leave her. Otherwise, she will be too far gone to help."

"I—can't—" Chelle choked through her tears.

"I understand," the soothsayer said slowly. "But if you don't, then she is doomed."

"By the gods, Chelle!" I shouted. "Get out of the way!"

Chelle held for a second, and then set Rose's body gently on the floor of the altar. "Okay. Okay. This had better work."

"There are no guarantees, but it is our last best hope." Shaina looked up at me. "Now, we need glass, big enough to cover the top of the vessel."

"Got it."

Behind the altar were two stained glass windows that Nimue had hidden under shrouds of black. I reached under the shrouds and smashed through one of the windows, picking up the fallen glass.

"This big enough?" I said as I held up the piece of blue glass.

Shaina nodded. "Yes. Now, when I say so, place the glass on top of the vessel, but not a moment before, okay?"

"Got it," I said, nodding.

The soothsayer and Shaina began to hum, and both of them glowed a light green. "Please stop your magic," the soothsayer said to Queen Aine. The fairy queen did so without question.

Rose began to break apart, turning into ashes, but the Soothsayer's humming grew in intensity, and the green light emanating from the soothsayer and Shaina wrapped around each flake of soot, and found every particle of Rose's soul floating through the hall.

"What are you doing?" Chelle said.

But the Soothsayer didn't speak. Her humming grew louder until the green light surrounded all of Rose's body, and then, with a flash, her corporeal form exploded into a million pieces of dust.

"No!" Chelle screamed, collapsing onto the altar. "You were supposed to save her!"

"Chelle!" I said. "Shut up!"

The humming had stopped, replaced by a mesmerizing chorus containing many more voices than the two that came from the Soothsayer and Shaina. As the music rose through the hall, so did the ashes of Rose. They swirled in the eddies of the air like a tornado before descending into the vase. Once every last particle of Rose was contained, Shaina turned to me.

"Now," she whispered.

I placed the glass over the vase and pushed it toward them. They raised their hands slowly onto either side of the vase and spoke in tandem. "Soul of the departed. You are bound to this vessel until such time as it fractures and breaks apart, or you are released."

With that, the vessel glowed a light blue for a moment, and then went dull.

"Is that it?" I asked. "Did it work?"

"Yes," the soothsayer said. "The bonding is complete, and successful. Rose's soul is here inside the vessel, though it will take some time before she learns to talk, and for us to construct a body for her."

Chelle crawled over to the vase. "But she's in there. All of her?"

"Yes," the soothsayer said.

Chelle picked up the vase. "Then I know what I have to do."

I knew what she meant to do. She meant to bring Rose to the Obsidian Spindle and send her home.

"Do you think it's even possible?" I asked.

"I don't know," she said, choking on the words. "But there's no way she would want to stay here like this if she could be back home."

"Then godspeed."

"Thank you."

CHAPTER 49

NIMUE

It smelled of rotten mung beans in the Obsidian Spindle. I expected some pomp and perhaps even a bit of circumstance as I ascended the dusty stairs up into the upper recesses of the Spindle, but aside from the cobwebs, all I got was a deep whiff of rotten mung bean. There were no windows, just jagged obsidian stairs and smooth obsidian walls.

The stairwell was steep and disappeared into the shadows above. It was a long time before I could even make out the top. As I climbed higher, I began to hear the crackling of a fireplace in the distance, and small waves of heat hit my face.

Eventually, I saw a doorway at the top of the tower with amber light emanating from it. The orange glow lit the steepled roof. I had reached the top.

Honestly, I was underwhelmed. I was about to meet the fates and have my question answered. I wanted something magical to happen to me the moment I entered the stairwell, and I had yet to see anything that matched the anticipation I'd felt for the last hundred years. I had interviewed hundreds of people about their experience inside the Spindle and wondered why none of them mentioned their time climbing the stairwell, and now I knew the answer was that it was completely unmemorable.

And tiring to boot. By the time I reached the top of the stairs, I was exhausted. Likely, that was the point of the exercise, since it gave the advantage to the witches waiting there.

"Are you here yet?" an old voice sounded.

"Don't rush her," another replied.

"Well, I'm bored," a third chimed in. "We haven't had a visitor in a long time, and the anticipation is killing me."

"Oh, that you were dead," the first voice grumbled. "To never have to hear your moaning again."

"Don't rush it."

"You'll miss it when it's gone."

"We'll see."

"Shortly."

The fates. I had waited so long for this moment, and I must have looked a dreadful fright. I moved my hands through my damp hair and took a deep breath.

"Come in, already," one of the crones said.

I stepped through the doorway. Three women sat in front of a roaring fire. I had studied them for years, anticipating this moment. Clotho, the youngest of the three, sat behind a loom, spinning thread. Lachesis took that thread and worked it into patches with a set of knitting needles. On the right, Atropos took the knitted patches and sewed them into a final quilt design upon which she sat. There were quilts piled high all along the room, which was huge. That I had expected, as well as the fact that all three were Gorgons, with their snakes hissing at me as I walked slowly into the room.

"Oh hush," Clotho said to the toothless snakes on her head.

Behind them, down a long hallway, stood a golden doorway lit with a light that seemed not to come from anywhere. It was the doorway back to Earth. I had seen pictures of it drawn from the memory of dreamers who had seen it, emblazoned with a long snake that wrapped around the entire width and length of it.

It was all so normal that once again, I felt almost let down. "Is this it?"

The three of them looked at each other, then laughed. No, they more than laughed. They cackled for a long while.

"Well, yes," Atropos said when the laughter stopped. "What did you expect?"

I furrowed my eyebrows as I thought of an answer. "The door to the Spindle has been closed for some time. I expected...something else. Anything else."

Lachesis's eyes met mine. "I'm sorry to be such a disappointment. It is enough for us, and that is all you can ask, in the end, right?"

"Forgive me," I said, averting my eyes. "You are the most powerful beings in Urgu. I simply meant that these humble accommodations are not worthy of your stature."

"Judge people by their stature, do you?" Clotho asked. "I judge them by their heart, and your heart has been so damaged it is hard to see through the walls you put up around it."

"So damaged," Atropos sighed. "And yet, there is still a glimmer of hope in it, child. Tell me, what would you ask of us?"

"I—I—" I couldn't get the words out. "I—would like to return to Earth."

The three looked at each other again, before Lachesis

gave a sad smile. "You must know that's not possible. We cut your thread long ago. There is simply no way."

"No, I refuse to believe that," I replied, tears forming in my eyes. "You are all powerful. You must—"

"No one is all powerful. We have our limitations just like everyone else. Only demons work in the kind of sorcery you are talking about."

I sneered. "Where can I find them, then?"

"In nightmares," Clotho said. "They are not the things of dreams, and so we do not parlay with them."

"They are the domain of Agrona, and Epilas."

"Lachesis!" Atropos snarled.

"Agrona?" I asked. "Wait, why Agrona?"

Lachesis looked at her sisters, and then back to me. "That is best taken up with her, if she will grant you an audience. Unfortunately, we must deny your request."

"Please, there must be something you can do."

"Yes," Clotho said grimly. "We can restore the power you once had before Hera took it away from you. That we can do."

"But we should not," Atropos said. "Because we know how you will use it."

"Horrible things will befall the universe if we give you back the power stolen from you."

"Screw the universe," I said, after thinking for a moment. "What has it ever done for me? I ask for my powers back. Let me prove to you that I will not use them for evil."

"Not evil," Clotho said. "Just misguided ambition. And death."

"I don't believe you," I sneered. "My fate is in my hands."

"No," Lachesis said. "It is in ours."

"However, we cannot deny you that request, should you make it."

"And this is my only wish ever to you?" I asked.

"Every soul gets one, and one only."

"Then, if I cannot return to Earth, I will take back my power."

The three sisters looked at each other and spoke as one. "Very well."

They chanted to themselves until their eyes glowed so bright I was nearly blinded. I squeezed my eyes shut, and when I did, my skin felt as if it were on fire. My body tensed and I fell to the ground. I screamed out in pain, and then, it was over, and a cool breeze washed over me.

I woke up and the light from the fire was dim, and so were the fates' eyes. "Did it work?"

"Try it."

"Fire." I looked down at my hands, and they lit as they once did. I had my powers back. "Ah ha! Wonderful."

"Yes," Lachesis said. "Wonderful, and terrible news."

"Not terrible. This is great!"

"For now," Clotho said, nodding. "However, you no longer have the blessing of a god, which means your body cannot stand so much raw power."

"What are you talking about?"

"You are wicked," Atropos said. "Down to your core, so we granted your wish, as we must, but only as we must. We gave you back your power, but while it will burn bright, it will burn fast, and in a matter of a month, your soul will burn away, into nothing."

"To prevent you from bringing your wickedness onto others," Lachesis said.

"And on the universe," Clotho added.

"What?" I looked down at my shaking hands. "How could you? I just want to go back to Earth. I'm not evil."

"The one place your soul must not go," Clotho said.

"The gods," I screamed. "They are so much worse than I am. Why don't you curse them?"

"They are not our problem," Atropos said, shaking her head. "They work on another plane. You, on the other hand, we can stop."

"NO!" I shouted. "LIGHTNING!"

Lightning fell out of my fingers and struck Atropos in the head, and she fell backwards. The other two fates' eyes glowed white, and when the lightning went to strike them, it rebounded back toward me.

"Shield!" A shield formed in front of me, and the lightning bounced to either side. "You will pay for this." I stalked toward the doorway.

"Better us," Clotho said.

"Than the universe," Lachesis replied.

And the light went out from the room as I leapt down the stairs and made my way toward the front door. If they were only going to give me a month, I had to make the most out of it. They told me that Agrona might be able to help me, and if that was the case, I would go to the mountains and speak to her myself.

CHAPTER 50
CHELLE

*Please be in there. Please be in there. Please be in there, Rose.
Please be in there.*

I pushed open the door to the bridge to the Obsidian
Spindle, clenching the urn that contained the remains of
my dear Rose.

Please don't die. Please don't die. Please don't die.

Even from halfway across the bridge, I could see the
door to the Obsidian Spindle was open, and I smiled.
Nimue had opened the door, and that meant she had done
something good in her life.

A screech filled the air, and the way forward was
blocked by a screaming seven-headed hydra. I had
forgotten about the seven-headed hydra. It was larger than
I remembered. Nearly as tall as the tower itself, and its
breath reeked of the rotten meat clinging to its teeth.

I placed the vase down and prepared for a fight, but that
was when Nimue flew out of the door and landed in front of
me with a loud thud.

"Sleep," she said, and the hydra crashed onto the
ground with a thud. I rushed to pick up the vase before the

shockwave knocked it over and shattered it into a million pieces.

"Thank you," I said.

"I don't care about you, little one," Nimue said. "My plans extend beyond you, now. Where is the golden book?"

"The book?"

"The one you stole from Hera."

"I don't know," I said. "I think it's inside Rose's room, on the desk. That's the last place it was."

"It better be there," Nimue growled, before she vanished. A moment later, she reappeared, now holding the book in her hands. "I'm sorry about Rose."

"Me too."

"I hope the fates are kinder to her than they were to me."

"Where will you go now?"

"To take my fate into my own hands."

And she vanished again, to the gods only know where. I carried the vase through the front door of the Spindle and held it as I climbed what seemed like several thousand jagged black stairs. The walls were unadorned and black. For as much fuss was made about it, I had expected more than just stairs.

When I reached the final landing, I found only a doorway, and the distinct sound of crying. Two different cries. I stepped through the doorway and found something I didn't expect. Two gorgons huddled around a third one, dead on the ground. All three of them were surrounded by an unfinished quilt.

"Excuse me?" I said as I took a step closer. "Are you...the fates?"

The youngest looking one turned to me. "There you are, my dear. It's so good to finally meet you."

"I'm sorry. Do I know you?"

"Not yet," the other one replied. "I am Lachesis."

"And I am Clotho," the other one said. Clotho pointed to the dead gorgon on the ground. "Unfortunately, you will never get to meet Atropos, the eldest of our kin."

"It's nice to meet you," I said, confused.

"You do not have to lie, dear." Lachesis said. "It is unbecoming."

"The fates don't lie," Clotho added. "We only tell the truth, horrible as it might be."

"Well, I'm not a fate, and where I'm from, we lie all the time."

Lachesis shook her head. "That will not do. If you are to become one of us, then you must never lie. Understood?"

"What are you talking about?" I said, indignant. "I'm not becoming one of you."

"She doesn't know," Clotho said.

"Of course she does not know," Lachesis sighed. "While we have been waiting for you a long time, you have only just met us. For us, this feels like meeting an old friend."

"What are you talking about?" I asked.

Clotho was walking away from me, towards a loom. "Events that were put in place decades ago, that are only coming to fruition now."

"Stop speaking in riddles!" I shouted.

"I'm sorry," Clotho said, sitting behind the loom. "It is our way."

Lachesis picked up two knitting needles and sat on a pillow on the floor. "You will get used to it."

"No, I won't. I'm not staying here. I'm trying to go home."

"Oh dear. You cannot go home. Nobody can go home.

Not without all three of the fates, and as you can see, there are only two."

"No, that's impossible," I held up the vase. "My girlfriend, Rose, I need to send her home. She has to go home."

"And she shall go home," Lachesis said. "We can make that happen."

"But you must join us."

"Yes...join us."

"Join...you?" I scoffed. "That's absurd. I'm not going to join you. I don't even know how to sew."

Clotho smiled. "You will learn."

"Atropos never learned to sew well, either," Lachesis added with a nod. "She just needed to complete what we have started, as do you."

"I—can't."

Lachesis grimaced. "Then your paramour will never return to Earth. Even now, her life force fades. We can feel it draining."

Clotho pulled up a thread from her loom. "This is her thread."

"And we are ready to cut it," Lachesis replied, picking up a pair of scissors.

"No!" I screamed, reaching out for it.

"There is little time," Lachesis said, inching the scissors closer to the string.

"There has to be another way," I said. Tears streamed down my face.

"We wish there was," Lachesis replied. "We did not want to lose our sister, either, but sacrifices must be made."

"Yes, sacrifices," Clotho added.

"But Rose will be okay?" I said. "If I do this? She can go back to Earth?"

"Those are two different questions," Clotho said,

pulling the string tight. "But she will go back to Earth, just like you wanted, and you will take a seat next to us."

Clotho moved closer to the string, as if utterly fascinated by it. "The other question, whether she will be fine, is less clear."

"She will be alive, though?" I asked.

"Alive," Lachesis said, moving her scissors until they were over top of the string. "Yes, alive, but not for long."

"Fine," I grumbled. "If that's the only way."

"It is the only way."

"Why are you doing this?" I asked.

"You are to play a role in what is to come."

"A role, yes. A big role, and we need you by our side for what is next."

I choked back tears. "Will I ever see her again?"

"We cannot say," Lachesis said. "That is against the rules."

"The path forward is hazy," Clotho added. "We can only pick out bits and pieces. We know only that your role is here."

"This sucks."

"You came into the Dream Realm to save your girlfriend, and in that, you will succeed. Clotho said. "Take solace in that."

"How do I do it? Return her to Earth, I mean."

Lachesis pointed the scissors away from the string and toward a golden door on the other side of the room adorned with a giant serpent. "Place the vase inside the golden door and then, come sit down next to us."

My feet were like lead as I walked to the door and pushed it open. There was nothing inside but blackness, but I did what I was told. I placed the vase down and closed the door.

"Goodbye, Rose."

Tears streamed down my face as I walked back toward the fates. The body of Atropos broke apart and her ashes floated around the room in a torrent before dissipating into the air.

"Here," Lachesis said. "This will be your first quilt."

She handed me a quilting square and I looked down at it. It was the face of a Gorgon. Lachesis and Clotho cried with me as I held up the quilt that their sister had died working on, and I knew that the quilt they knit was for her.

"This is your sister," I said, shocked.

"Yes," Clotho said.

"Sacrifices all around," Lachesis replied, placing a bony hand on my shoulder.

"What do I do?"

"Take the needle and sew it next to the others."

I nodded. I didn't know how to sew, but I sat down and took a threaded needle out of the pin cushion next to me.

"Small loops," Clotho said.

"Tightly," Lachesis added.

I took the needle and sewed the thread into the existing quilt that lay under me, binding them together. "You knew she would die?"

"We all knew, even her, but it was the only way."

"Only way for what?"

"Only way this all doesn't end."

"Oh."

"And Rose?" I said with a deep swallow.

Clotho took a deep breath and closed her eyes. "She is already gone."

In the distance, I heard a door slam shut, and knew I was now locked into my fate with no way out.

CHAPTER 51

ROSE

I gasped for air as I shot up in bed.

Am I alive?

Yes, I was alive. *How was I alive?*

The last thing I remembered was being stabbed in the back.

I heard the beep of a heart monitor. As my eyes focused, I saw the faces of the two people I wanted to see least in the whole world: my mother and father.

"Oh my god," my mom said, tears in her eyes. "My little Rosebud? Is that you?"

Chelle had done it. She had brought me home. She had saved me, like she always wanted, and now I was back on Earth, just like she promised. I looked into my heart, trying to find a way to feel about it, but I felt nothing.

Absolutely nothing.

I was numb.

And now, I was alone.

Utterly alone.

And completely powerless.

Just like I always had been.
This sucked.

EPILOGUE
NIMUE

A lightning storm covered the mountains as I flew toward Agrona's palace. There were no stars. I had never seen darkness like this.

Something moved in the treetops below me, making its way through the trees, slowly snapping branches underneath its lumbering hands. It was enormous, and its cry echoed through the sky. Something was making its way through Urgu, and not even the gods were prepared for it.

The smell of sulfur grew thicker as I made my way closer to the castle. Every time the lightning cracked, I could make out its outline, and I felt the presence of massive beasts roaming beneath me, descending from the mountains. The wind tried its best to keep me away, blowing me off course, and choking my lungs, but I was undeterred. I would speak with Agrona if it was the last thing I did.

Finally, I reached the gnarled castle that Agrona called home, high atop the highest mountain, where even her most devoted followers could not tread. Her castle was cut into the rock of the mountain itself, with a great, jagged mouth as the entrance, a dewy tongue for the door.

I hid my disgust and pushed open the sticky door. Inside, I was met by a long black hallway, with lighted torches on the blood-red walls. Every step I took, the whole mountain creaked and groaned. I wanted to go back. I wanted to go home.

But I couldn't. The fates let slip that Agrona held the key to me returning to Earth, and they hadn't given me much time to find answers, so I had to keep moving forward with whatever clues I was given.

The lightning crashed again, but this time it was inside the castle. As I reached the end of the long hallway, I saw a massive portal filled with crackling blue electricity, reaching all the way to the top of the throne room. It spewed lightning into the air, and lit the whole room with its energy.

Next to the portal, at the end of the long carpet, sat a woman on a throne made of mountain rocks. She wore pelts of bears around her body, and a crown of bone. Her eyes glowed white as her hair, while the rest of her body was shrouded in darkness.

"Agrona?" I asked.

"Who dares disturb me?" the voice shrieked.

I took a step forward. "It is I, Nimue, Wicked Witch of the West, ruler of Oz, consort to Hera until she shunned me, and I am here to pledge my allegiance to you."

"I have no need for it from one who has failed so mightily and so often."

"Please," I said. "I brought you an offering." I held out the golden book of Hypnos. "This book will reveal every secret of Urgu to one who can read it."

Agrona cocked her head and snatched the book out of

the air without moving. It moved across the room to her and she caught it in her hand. She felt the book for a moment, before cocking a wry smile.

"This pleases me. What is it you need?"

"I wish to receive your blessing."

"I have never blessed anyone, and don't plan to start now. I need every bit of my power for what is to come."

"Please, the fates told me the answers can be found in you. If I don't receive your blessing I will d—"

"The fates? So, the Spindle is open again?"

"Yes."

"Wonderful. Then the next phase of our plan can begin."

"Please, I only wish to return to Earth."

"As do I," Agrona said. "The time is close for Urgu to fall."

"I don't have much time left."

Agrona turned to the portal. "You can take your plea up with Epialas."

"Epialas? God of Nightmares? But he resides in the Nightmare Realm."

"Not for long." Agrona held her hand up. "Soon, my love will join me here."

"Epialas? Here?"

"His brother is weak and has abandoned this place. Epialas is strong, and when he has conquered this land, he will set us all free."

"Free?"

"With fire and stone," Agrona said.

"I cannot wait that long," I replied, sheepishly. I only had a month left to make my peace and find a way back to Earth.

"Here, there is nothing but time. Old wounds turn new again with the passage of the eons."

"Not for me. I must return to Earth now."

"There are no answers here."

"If not here, then where?"

"There are no answers here—"

"I know!"

"However, there may be answers beyond," Agrona said as if I hadn't interrupted her, again gesturing to the portal. "I am bound here until my love frees me, or joins me, but you may enter the Nightmare realm. Find my love and bring him to me."

"The Nightmare Realm?" I said, swallowing as I stepped closer to the portal. "That's where this leads?"

"Yes," Agrona replied. "The answers you seek may be found within, or it might drive you mad."

I nodded. "I'm willing to take that chance."

"You agree to find my love, and bring him to me?"

"I do."

"Then, the gods' speed to you."

I stepped into the Nightmare Realm.

You finished The Wicked Witch, book 2 in the Obsidian Spindle Saga. If you loved this book, please consider leaving a review on your favorite storefront. Reviews are the best way for me to see if people want me to continue a series.

If you like *The Wicked Witch,* keep reading after the author's note for a preview of the third book in the series, *The Fairy Queen.*

Author's Note

While the first book in the Obsidian Spindle Saga took something like two years to move from thought to words on a page, the second book flowed out of me quickly in the matter of a couple weeks during November of 2019. It took forever to figure out where to put all the main characters, and make them fit together, but once I had their starting positions in the first book, all the dominos started to fall over.

By the time I finished the first book, I was desperate to start the second one. I knew I wanted to focus on Nimue, and her loss of power. One of my favorite animated shows, *Niko and the Sword of Light*, had a plot where the main magician lost their powers and had to figure out how to live as a human, and I thought it would be a great thing to see Nimue deal with in the second book.

After all, she's used to being rich and powerful. What would happen if she was brought low? I hope you enjoyed finding out. I really enjoyed her struggle, and hope it showed a bit of her humanity after a first book where she played little more than a foil to Chelle and Rose.

One thing that I was surprised about in this story was that Rose returned to Earth in this book, instead of the end of book 3, as I originally planned. However, I had just spent this entire book inside the Dream Realm, and I needed somebody to return to Earth. This series is supposed to happen both on Earth and in the Dream Realm, after all, and I really needed to get back there with at least one point of view character. The only logical choice was Rose.

If Chelle returned to Earth it would mean the quest was over, and Nimue couldn't return either because she is merely a soul without a vessel. Red doesn't seem to want to leave Urgu, even if given the choice, and since this whole series has been about Rose returning to Earth with the help of Chelle, it gave the story a leg to stand on, and a big relief at the end of this book.

Since this book series doesn't wrap up all its threads at the end of each book, I feel the need to include a BIG CLIMAX, which will keep you satisfied that this was a complete thought, while dying to come back for more.

Rose returned to Earth in this one, but what will happen to her there? How will Nimue deal with the demons in the Nightmare Realm? Who will take over the throne of Oz? These are all questions that you'll find out in *The Fairy Queen,* the third book in the Obsidian Spindle Saga.

If you like *The Wicked Witch,* keep reading for a preview of the third book in the series, *The Fairy Queen.*

THE FAIRY QUEEN PREVIEW

Book 3 of the Obsidian Spindle Saga
By:
Russell Nohelty

Edited by:
Leah Lederman

Proofread by:
Katrina Roets

Cover by:
JV Arts

AINE

Everyone of royal blood needed to die before my reign as queen over the Land of Oz could truly begin. Every single one of Nimue's sycophants would have to be disposed of so we didn't have a repeat of what happened to Rose, the last queen. I would not be assassinated. I'd lived too long and seen too much to get taken down like that.

"You can't do this!" Cyrano said, tears falling down his long, ugly nose. His piteous, bloodshot eyes stared at me with a combination of contempt and nervousness.

"I can do whatever I want," I snarled. "I am the queen. Or have you forgotten that already?"

Cyrano and his accomplices were responsible for Rose's death. She'd only been queen for about eleven seconds before they killed her, and I wouldn't let them get away with it. She was my friend. The ancillary benefit was that their deaths led me directly to the most powerful throne in Urgu, but that was just a fortuitous coincidence.

"Please," Odysseus sobbed. He was the tall and strapping master of war, crying like a child. Even hundreds of years of life didn't prepare him for his own death. "Have some heart."

I nearly laughed. "Did you have heart when you plotted to kill the rightful queen of Oz?"

I had already sent the council of bishops from the Church of the Six to their deaths over the edge of the royal balcony. Ozma, a previous queen, used to address her adoring subjects there. That was before she was usurped and then eventually thrown from the same balcony by the one who had deposed her, the wicked witch. Nimue.

The council, along with the Church's leader, had led the charge to kill Rose. Grand Pious Edwina plunged the dagger into the poor girl's back herself, and then had the audacity to smile afterward. They had to die first, to send a message. Nobody dared kill the clergy. After all, the Church of the Six served all Urgu, not just the Land of Oz, and I had wiped them off the face of the continent with nary a second thought.

Once the bishops were gone, I had dusted the entirety of the royal court for all the Emerald City to witness. They cheered for it. The Church of the Six was an antiquated institution and the nobles had held down the masses for too long. Now, all that was left for me to do was to finish the small council and then I could start rebuilding the Land of Oz.

"We didn't mean to do it." Antonio, master of coin, sniffled as he looked at the crowd of Ozians screaming for his head. "We were doing what was best for Oz!"

"Don't insult my intelligence," I spat back at him. "I was a queen since before I came to this place and have ruled the Enchanted Woods for centuries. Do you really think I know not how to take care of conspirators?" I knew the people demanded blood. They craved it. Nimue knew that, and I had tried to impart that advice to Rose, but the girl didn't believe me, and it led to her death. She was too kind-hearted to rule.

"We didn't—" Cyrano almost lost his footing from atop the railing where he stood precariously. "We weren't..."

"What?" I asked. Rose was my only friend, the only person who had treated me kindly in decades, and I would have my revenge for her. I would solidify my rule. "Expect to be caught?"

"We were just doing what was best for Oz," Odysseus pleaded, snot bubbling in his nose. "Can't you see that?"

"Yes, I can see that you truly believe the lie," I said, floating above them. My small size would have been comical compared to their stature if I didn't ooze power from every pore. I knew how to command a room. We fae had to learn quickly about the true dastardly nature of humans passed down from generation to generation. If we didn't, we would be subject to witness it firsthand. "The worst part is that you won't admit your treachery and die with dignity."

I looked each counselor in the eye, the purple of my robes reflected in each conspirator's face. My mother thought that my choice of purple would make me look soft, but I knew it projected royalty. "And wasn't it convenient that what was best for Oz happened to be the best for your coffers?"

"That was a coincidence!" Antonio shouted. "The girl could not rule. You saw it. She was a child, and an outsider. She had no knack for—"

"We were all outsiders once!" I bellowed. "She was chosen by Hypnos himself, and decreed to rule by divine right until..." The thought of Rose's body deteriorating into ash stopped me, momentarily. I lifted my chin, maintaining my air of invincibility. I could not choke up, not now. And there was nothing more to say. I gave a nod to the Mountain People who held sharp lances to the backs of the former small council. "Drop them."

The Mountain People that Red and Chelle rescued from the Gates of Droangor proved to be most loyal after Rose's assassination. They were instrumental in rounding up the nobles who begged sanctuary from the Queen's Guard and provided insulation from the Queen's guard that was still inexplicably loyal to Nimue. Plus, their monstrous appearance made even the most battle-hardened soldier quiver. Those that plotted murder thought twice before crossing me, as I had my own army of elite soldiers protecting me.

My Mountain soldiers turned their glowing eyes to me and nodded back. They pushed their lances into the backs of the sniveling conspirators, who fell off the balcony with a collective scream. They tumbled through the air and smashed against the ground, breaking into a million pieces of ash on the cobblestone courtyard.

I watched the citizens of the Emerald City cheering as the men's ashes floated into the air. "Justice for your queen!" I shouted, and again the crowd erupted with cheers. They chanted my name, over and over again. The rapturous joy on their faces proved their loyalty to me. I rode into their hearts on the strings of Rose's kind soul. The common people loved Rose for toppling the Wicked Witch and were heartbroken when she was murdered.

In their grief, I brought stability. I had mentored Rose and trained her to become a queen during her short days on the throne. They knew me as a fair, if not feared ruler, and I swore to bring justice to their beloved queen. Yes, I took the throne when Rose died, but the people of Oz let me keep it. I was their queen. There was no one besides me who had a claim to it, since I'd killed all of them. Until Hypnos appointed a new ruler—which had taken over a hundred years the last time around—I would rule the land.

"A new era of wonder has begun!" I shouted to the crowd. "Long live the Emerald City!"

The throne of Oz had never been my birthright, but its power was something I coveted in my youth. The Enchanted Woods had its charm, but Oz was the most powerful province in Urgu, and in lieu of escaping the Dream Realm outright, it was a fine prize. Where Rose, the Dreamer, had failed to control the nobles, and the Wicked Witch had failed to open the Obsidian Spindle, I would be successful. I had secured justice for Rose, my friend, and now I would journey through the Obsidian Spindle to my destiny, my return to Earth.

I had seen the door open once, only once, for a single shining moment when the Gorgon, Chelle, walked inside it with her beloved Rose's ashes. The door shut behind her. Now I knew it could be opened with the right spell, and Nimue knew the spell. I would find her, even if it took a century, and make my way back to Earth, and away from Urgu forever.

"*FAIRY!*" a voice boomed. "*Meet your end.*"

Black ooze inked through the sky like oil creeping across water, until the sky was sackcloth black and the wind began to howl. Below, the citizens of Oz screamed and fled in all directions. We had all heard the voice before.

Hera.

She was on her way to destroy the land of Oz and take the Obsidian Spindle by force. An onyx mist rose into the air and crashed through the street like a tidal wave, sweeping up my subjects in its wake.

Shadow Demons. Hera controlled them. They would

destroy everything. I would be nothing but a queen of ashes.

Before Rose died, she had raised the defenses on the castle. No magical being that meant to do me harm could enter the castle without my permission.

I just had to hope it was powerful enough to keep out a god.

CHELLE

Bang!

  Bang!

  Bang!

My fists had been scraped raw from slamming them against the door to the Obsidian Spindle for hours, but the door wouldn't budge, even an inch. My blood smeared across the oaken door as I slammed against it. "Let me out!

"*Magna augue!*" I shouted. A fireball swelled between my hands. It grew to the size of a basketball before I pushed it out toward the door, where it exploded without leaving so much as a scratch. I smelled my burning blood as it dissipated, mixed with the sweet smell of smoke as the remnants of the extinguished flame floated into the darkness of the Spindle that was my prison.

"*Fulgur inspiratione!*" A blue shock of lightning grew from my fingertips, and I flung it at the door like I was Emperor Palpatine. The lightning shook my hands, but I didn't let up for a full minute, and when I was done, the only thing left to show my effort was a black stain of electricity on the door.

There was no way to open the door back to Urgu. Between my endless sessions sewing the Quilt of Life together with the other fates, Clotho and Lachesis, I would come to the door and try to open it, desperate to end my obligation to the Gorgon women who held me in the Obsidian Spindle.

"I am a hostage," I muttered.

"You aren't a hostage," I heard from behind me. I turned to see Clotho standing on the black stairs, her ancient snakes coiled silently around her head. She smiled at me. "If you were a hostage, then we would send for ransom from somebody who cares about you. The only two who care about you here are my sister and me. And you are not a prisoner either, since you chose to remain here with us."

"Semantics." It was true, though: I had entered a contract with them and become a fate after their sister Atropos was murdered by Nimue. That crazy witch opened the Obsidian Spindle for the first time in a century, and what did she do but kill one of the fates?

"We are also stuck here, and that is an appropriate term. The three of us, stuck together, after having made a choice."

Only a Gorgon could become a fate, and I just happened to be Gorgon enough to fit the bill after the death of their sister, Atropos. Wrong place at the wrong time, or right place at the right time, depending on how you looked at it, and who was doing the looking.

"I just want to go home."

"You are home," Clotho said, sweetly. I liked her more than her ornery sister, but I saw myself in Lachesis. I think she saw herself in me, too, which was why she was so hard on me. Clotho was kind.

It was an easy choice, to become a fate, because it saved

Rose, the woman I loved more than life itself, and sent her back to Earth. If I hadn't made that choice, the door back to Earth couldn't be opened, and Rose would be damned to ashes for eternity.

Now, at least she was back on Earth where she was safe and could live a real life. I would die for that girl, so the least I could do was suffer through the mindless tedium of sewing the Quilt of Life for an epoch or two.

"I hate it here."

"That's how it felt for us, too," Clotho said. "But in time, you grow to love the isolation, and the quiet." Clotho held her hand out. "Come, we have a surprise for you."

"I've seen your surprises," I replied. "I haven't liked one yet."

I looked down at my fingers, bloody and raw from a combination of banging on the door to the Spindle and working the needle and thimble for days on end. Gingerly, I placed my hand in hers.

"You will like this one, I believe," Clotho said. She led me up the stairs.

That was how it had been since I came to them. They asked questions as statements and expected me to follow them blindly. I had never followed anything blindly in my entire life. I never believed in the will of gods, or the fickle finger of fate, even though I was now one of them.

I was no willing subject. I meant what I said. The fact that I couldn't leave meant I was a prisoner. Even though I had made this choice, I regretted it. Only thoughts of Rose made it worthwhile, and the belief that she was safe. I held onto those thoughts and that belief every time the regret overwhelmed me.

"None have ever taken the mantle of fate willingly,"

Clotho said, walking up the dark stairwell that led to the Spindle's only room at the top. That was where Clotho spun the thread of another lonely soul bound for the afterlife, and Lachesis knit it into a patch. It was my job to take the patch and sew it into the Quilt of Life.

"Why did you choose to stay?" I asked Clotho.

"Similar to you, actually," she replied. "Though it was a boy. He was very sick, and my sacrifice kept him alive, for a time. They all die, eventually. I remember the day Lachesis weaved his patch, just like she weaved those of the ones she had loved and hoped to save. It was the last time I shed a tear until the death of my sister."

"That's sad," I replied.

"Quite," Clotho nodded. "But in time, I grew to love the work. It is important, and there are so few truly important jobs. I take satisfaction in that, and in the simple act of remembering the dead, and my part in all of it."

"That doesn't sound like much," I said.

"It's not much, but it is all we have." Clotho walked into the room. When I followed, she sat to the left of her sister, Lachesis, who was silently putting another patch together. Next to her was a stack of patches, waiting for me. I looked down at them. Maybe she was right. Maybe there was joy in it, at least in the duty of it. Each of those pieces represented a life, and their memory would always live on in the Quilt of Life.

"Sit," Clotho said with a smile.

I shook my head. "I don't know if I can sew any more today."

"That is not your choice," Lachesis said. Her voice was hoarse. "Sit. Down."

She treated me like a mule to break, and it often took all

of my willpower not to burn her to ash like Nimue had done to her sister. "You talk a big game for an old woman. Remember, I have a body, which makes me the most powerful thing in this room. I could take you both."

I was the only being in all Urgu with a body. Everyone else came through in their dreams, as a soul, or as the result of an overactive imagination, but I came through a door guarded by Mydnyte, a servant of Nox, the goddess of darkness.

Clotho chuckled. "You should not underestimate us, but we will not force you. Nothing will force you, but a feeling, deep in your soul, will compel you to finish the job we started, eventually."

"You mock everything we stand for," Lachesis added. "Atropos—"

"Died," I said. "She died to make room for me. I know. And you hate it. I know that. I still don't understand why, though."

Clotho smiled. "We will tell you. But first, we have a gift for you."

I eyed her suspiciously. "I don't know what you could give me that I want."

"We have many powers you have not seen," Lachesis said.

"And we will teach you one," Clotho said. "We will teach you how to reach out and see your beloved."

"Rose?" An excited shudder rolled through me.

"Yes," Lachesis said. "But be warned. Do not dwell in the land of the living, or you will be lost, and see things that you do not wish to see. The memories will wash over you, and you will be overwhelmed by what you will witness."

"I can handle it," I said. "I've seen—"

"You've seen nothing," Lachesis snapped. "Atropos was wrong to give up her life for you, and Clotho is wrong to keep you close. You are far too hot-headed for the work we require."

"But she is perfect for what will come next," Clotho said. "It has been foreseen."

"What is next?" I asked, throwing my hands in the air. I had pieced together enough to know that something big was coming, and I had a part in it. "Will you please just tell me instead of talking in riddles?"

"Soon," Clotho replied. "But first, we will show you that which you seek above all else."

I sat down on the mat next to Lachesis. What I wanted more than anything was to see Rose, and if this was a chance, I would listen.

"Close your eyes," Lachesis said. I did.

"Reach out with your feelings and think of Rose. Think of her and let your feelings for her wash over you. Let the most powerful memory of your time together drown you in its happiness."

I thought back to the first time Rose ever saw the snakes that hissed above my head. I was as frightened as I had ever been. Fighting legions of monster hunters didn't make me a fraction as nervous as I was when I came out to her as a monster. No mortal human had ever seen my greatest shame—my truest self. What if she recoiled in horror? I would be forced to start a new life.

But she didn't scream or run away. She simply smiled, and touched them each in turn, sweetly, before turning to me. "They're beautiful," she said. "And so are you."

Tears flowed down my face, and suddenly the dark behind my eyes washed away, and Rose's face stared back at me. Not the memory of Rose, but her actual face. I don't know how I could tell that it wasn't a memory, or a hallucination, but I knew it was real. She was alive, and she was okay.

For the first time in days, I smiled.

ROSE

I wanted to hate myself, my life. I wanted to hate Chelle. I wanted to hate something; anything. Even the littlest thing in the whole world.

But I didn't. I couldn't.

I didn't hate anything. I didn't love anything, either. I didn't feel...anything. Ever since returning from the Dream Realm, I hadn't felt one iota of pain or joy. I had no feelings about moving back in with my parents, or having to commute to school, or selling the van that Chelle and I lived in for almost a year. It still smelled like her when I dropped it off.

I almost thought I could feel something then for a fleeting moment, but as quickly as the feeling came upon me, it drifted away. Even that feeling, strong as it should have come to wrecking me, never came too close to the surface. It was like a distant acquaintance on a faraway beach, waving to you from the horizon. You could place a hint of recognition on their face, but you had no real memory of them. That was how the most intense feeling came upon me now.

All I could do was look upon my life with dispassionate inhumanity, as if I wasn't the one living my life, but a bystander watching a boring movie, hoping for it to be over soon. I barely recognized myself in the mirror. My eyes were dull and colorless, except for the blood red veins that splintered from my irises. My dark blonde hair fell onto my face like an ugly mat, and I barely had the energy to brush it away before turning from the mirror and putting on a pair of dirty blue jeans to compliment my stained t-shirt.

I had to take on summer school so that I didn't fall behind on my class load. The world had moved on, even if mine came to a dead stop when I fell into that diabetic coma. It seemed like a lifetime ago I'd been in Urgu.

All in all, I had been in the Dream Realm for less than a month. Upon my return, it took the rest of the semester before I felt well enough to venture outside the house, and by then I had registered an incomplete in all my classes.

At least going to school got me out of the house.

I stepped out of the double wide trailer I shared with my parents and out into the yard, if you could call it that. It was mostly a dirt patch with two fold-out chairs and a small grill we sometimes used to cook hot dogs.

"Off so soon?" my mother said, coming around the side of the trailer where she was hanging clothes on the line. I didn't need to be able to feel to remember that I hated her. The memories were strong with the misery she put me through. Still, it was only the memory of a feeling, and not the feeling itself.

"Yeah," I said. "Got class."

My parents agreed to add me back to their insurance when I told them that Chelle was gone. Luckily, too, otherwise I would have to pay tens of thousands of dollars in medical bills for my stay in the hospital. They never let me forget it. Every time I tried to avoid them, they made sure I knew that the only reason I wasn't drowning in debt was because of them.

"Don't be too late," Mom said. "I worry. You know, after what we went through this year."

As if them kicking me out of their house was my fault. It wasn't my fault I was gay. It was their fault they disowned me because of it, and now they thought that because Chelle is stuck in the Dream Realm it meant I wasn't gay anymore, like they can just sweep it all under the rug.

Out of sight, out of mind I guess, and I would never tell them differently. I would never tell them anything ever again. I needed a place to stay for now, but once I could pull my life together, I was gone, forever.

"I won't," I lied. I had no idea when I would be home. Hopefully, I would never come home again.

Mom's eyes narrowed. "I got next month's insulin for you when you get back."

Insulin. I needed it, and it cost hundreds of dollars a month without their insurance. I tried to live without it once...and I ended up in a diabetic coma, clinging to life, while my soul was stuck in the Dream Realm.

"K," I said with all the passion I could muster, which was basically none. The implication was clear: If I didn't come home early, I wouldn't get my medicine. If I didn't get my medicine, I would die. Great mom. Little did she know I had a stash that I kept at school in case I decided to run away and never come back. I used the cash from selling the van to make sure I had an escape plan.

I wished that I could fry her with a bolt of lightning, or a fireball, or manipulate her mind, but I no longer had powers. Chelle saw to that when she sent me back to Earth. I was back to being a nothing burger from nowhereville, instead of a Queen with magic bestowed by the gods...and the worst part of it all was that I didn't even have Chelle. She left me alone, in worse shape than when I left.

A twinge of hatred washed over me, then blew away as fast as it came. I was left alone with my nothingness, staring at my mother. I jumped into the beat-up Civic hatchback I'd bought with the money from the van—what was left after buying an emergency stash of insulin—and lumbered off down the dirt road.

If you liked that preview, then pick up *The Fairy Queen* today.

ALSO BY RUSSELL NOHELTY

The Obsidian Spindle Saga

The Godsverse Chronicles

Ichabod Jones: Monster Hunter

Cthulhu is Hard to Spell

My Father Didn't Kill Himself

Sorry for Existing

Gumshoes: The Case of Madison's Father

The Invasion Saga

The Vessel

Worst Thing in the Universe

The Void Calls Us Home

The Marked Ones

The Little Bird and the Little Worm

Gherkin Boy

Find a complete list at

https://www.russellnohelty.com/books/

ABOUT THE AUTHOR

Russell Nohelty is a USA Today bestselling author, publisher, and speaker. He is the author of dozens of novels and graphic novels including The Godsverse Chronicles, The Obsidian Spindle Saga, and Ichabad Jones: Monster Hunter. He has a very entertaining newsletter, which you can join at www.russellnohelty.com. He lives in Los Angeles with his wife and dogs.

Get one of my favorite books for free at:
    www.russellnohelty.com/mail
    Substack:
    https://authorstack.substack.com
    Bookbub:
    https://www.bookbub.com/profile/russell-nohelty